I0630932

What readers are saying about...
The One-Eyed Man

Stinton's *The One-Eyed Man* positively shimmers with multi-layered characters—seers, prophets, feelers, readers—they populate the pages of a narrative woven with mystery and intrigue. With fascinating world building and an engaging pace, this Hamal story will not disappoint. Perhaps like me, by the end of this book, you will want to sit down and share a steaming cup of tea with Hamal, Cale, Justice, and Cedrick.

— Catherine Posey, PhD
www.bookish-illuminations.com

The character of Hamal is very endearing. I love how the story develops and new characters are added. They each have a significant role. I eagerly awaited this book because the first one was so good, and I wasn't disappointed. From a ministry standpoint, these books make me wonder why these things can't be true in the kingdom. There are truths in these books that you can apply to your life.

— Sue Frisbie
Northwest Gathering Center
Coeur d'Alene, Idaho

Lauren Stinton has outdone herself with the latest Hamal story, *The One-Eyed Man*. Winsome and funny, deep yet entertaining, she weaves a web of characters that will make you laugh and cry and most importantly long for a world where wisdom and humility are honored as much as they are in King's Barrow. Where all people and their gifts are accepted and seen for their value because of their differences instead of in spite of them. Where faith is as simple as Hamal's. No hidden agendas, no distrust, no need to control— simple trust that if you follow Wisdom, things will work out right. I loved this journey and trust that you will, too!

— John E. Thomas
President, Streams Ministries

What readers are saying about...
The Hamal Books

No library should be devoid of Hamal or his humble, healing hands. An extraordinary fantasy ride for all ages, this tale draws readers in from the first page of the first book and leaves them wanting more and more at the conclusion of the second. As the story unfolds, so does one's admiration for Hamal with his simple way of seeing the world (and himself). And as the story grows so does Hamal's confidence in his abilities as a healer and his realization that he truly has a decisive role in his enchanting world.

— Amanda Allpress
Teen Services Librarian

In an era where fantasy writing has become fairly predictable, Lauren Stinton surprises us with what I would call "fresh fantasy." The Hamal Books introduce us to a unique world in which people are distinguished by a set of supernatural attributes that determine their roles and relationship with one another. It is against this backdrop that Hamal arises as a humble yet powerful hero, bringing justice and goodness to the world around him. Hamal is pure inspiration.

— Michael Brodeur, Author
Destiny Finder
Revival Culture

I have never read a book with a protagonist like Hamal. How can his character be so unique, yet so easy to identify with? I love that double-meaning line, "I always leave scars." Yeah, he's talking about his healing capabilities. But I think we can all relate to that feeling: that we ruin what we touch, that we can't do anything right, that we are good, but never great. Hamal's story is one that will have something for everyone, I think. I can't wait for the next book!

— Rachel Nace
@never_too_many_books

Hamal is the kind of guy I would like to be. Wise, full of surprising insight, yet easy to get to know. Lauren's depiction of Hamal and his world brings out all kinds of good possibilities, with her description of the gifts in each person, and how they relate to each other (think: your blood and bones can talk, tell stories of what they've seen). Lauren writes in such a way that it seems *Should I Choose to Die Again* was a "why didn't I ever think of that" moment in almost every chapter. If you like Christian fantasy and yet have a solid grounding in the Word of God, this book is a delightful read!

— Ken Lindberg
California

Other books by Lauren Stinton

The Hamal Books:
Should I Choose to Die Again
www.thehamalbooks.com

The House of Elah series:
The House of Elah
The Alusian's Quest
The King's Man

THE ONE-EYED MAN

For Steve and Jane

THE ONE-EYED MAN

A HAMAL NOVEL BY

LAUREN STINTON

For here the
earth breathes
— Shel Galen —
from his
History of Earth and Soil

THERAINE

Thalbrake Mountains

Crimson Bay

West Sea

Dhalbou Jungle

Table of Contents

1 What Happened Today in The King's Council

Hamal didn't mean to gasp. The moment it happened, he clamped his hand across his mouth and ducked down in his chair. But it was too late. The king fell silent, and every person—every man and every woman—in the large room turned to look at Hamal, who felt heat jump through his face. His first council meeting with the king had started less than a minute ago, and he had interrupted it almost as soon as he had given his greeting.

His friend Cale Lehman leaned close to him and asked in a low voice, "What is it, Hamal?"

Hamal shifted awkwardly in his chair and then twisted around so he could whisper in Cale's ear. Cale tilted his head, giving Hamal clear access. "I was just wondering where the feelers are."

"The feelers?"

"Aye." Hearing the strange note in Cale's voice, Hamal pulled back to see his friend's face and looked at him with a frown. "Doesn't the king have feelers on his council?"

He pointed at the little triangular nameplate that stood in front of him. The other side in neat letters declared his name and his gift. "I can see that several other gifts are here, but I can't see any feelers. This is a meeting about South Barrow and trying to help the people who live there in poverty. There are a lot of feelers living in poverty in South Barrow."

Cale studied Hamal's face, his look contemplative, like he was trying to choose his words carefully. "You think such a council meeting should have feelers in attendance?"

"I think every council meeting should have feelers in attendance."

"Ah." Cale leaned back in his chair and raised his voice as he addressed the king. "Your majesty, the sage would like to know where the feelers are among your council."

Murmurs went around the table. Every chair was filled, and there were many chairs, more than Hamal could count easily, but none of them held feelers.

King Cedrick looked around the room for a moment before bringing his heavy gaze back to Hamal. Breathing a sigh, the king said bluntly, "I don't have feelers on my council, Hamal. They are good people. Many of them are noble to a fault, but they tend to find matters of government overwhelming. We have not had a feeler on any governmental council in King's Barrow in generations." The king grimaced. "And I can see from your expression that you find this peculiar. Very well. If wisdom finds something peculiar with my council, I will hear him out." He waved his hand. "Please—on your feet. Address us."

Hamal could feel the eyes of everyone in the room, even the guards at the doors, as he scooted his padded chair away from the table and slowly stood up. He had never "addressed" a king's council before. He had spoken to Cedrick in private several times, and he'd even had conversations with many of the council members, but this felt unusual to him—trying to speak to everyone at once.

"Your majesty," he began. It was always good to be polite with kings in public, even if they liked to tease you in private. Cedrick, to Hamal's surprise, enjoyed teasing people when he wasn't surrounded by what Cale called his "surly council members." Hamal took a deep breath. "This is a meeting to make South Barrow better." He turned to Cale. "Isn't that what you said? You said we were meeting to help South Barrow."

Cale nodded. "Yes. This is a meeting to discuss how the Ministry of Education could improve their programs and aid within South Barrow. The ministry is made up entirely of readers and growers, in that order. They are sitting there."

He gestured to several men and women at the distant end of the table. One of the women lifted her hand in something resembling a small wave, and Hamal decided it was a wave and waved back.

"Everyone else at the table is a member of the king's council," Cale continued, "with a variety of gifts at their disposal. However, none of them are feelers. Hamal, why don't you tell the council what you know about feelers?" Cale's eyes, silver and intense, came to focus somewhere just above Hamal's right ear. He used his gift, and then his lips moved in a slight smile. "Pretend we're little children who have never heard of feelers. How would you explain their gift and function?"

As everyone else started whispering to one another, Hamal asked Cale, "Now?"

The seer nodded. "Now."

Hamal thought for a moment, trying to decide where to start. "This is what I know. I know that many gifts have forgotten that the feeler gift is strong. It is powerful because you can do things with feelers to make other things happen. It depends on what you want—and the feeler's name. It all depends on the feeler's name. If you want to make certain that all your decisions are kind and generous, then you find a feeler with a name like *Kindness* or

Love, and you give him a job."

Hamal looked around at the council members. "You make him part of your council. If you want to make certain that all your decisions are wise, then you find a feeler with that name, like *Wisdom* or *Knowledge* or *Understanding*. Feelers influence people. They're like wind that can come along and stir things. They don't even have to say anything—if you give them a job and put them in that job, that's what they'll do. They will influence people according to their names. A feeler's name is important. And it's very important that feelers are given jobs. They need to be in charge of things."

No one said anything.

Cale was smiling broadly, though Hamal wasn't certain why. "So you think it is important that feelers—certain feelers, certain names—be a part of the king's council as we seek to change the fortune of South Barrow."

"Oh, especially then," Hamal cried. "Think about all the horrible things that have happened in South Barrow! People are worn down and scared and frightened all the time, and they can't read or write, and some of them don't know how to get jobs, or how to keep them once they have them, and they don't understand wisdom."

Hamal gestured toward the king. "King Landan, Cedrick's father, made slavery illegal ten years ago, and South Barrow is where the one-time slaves went if they couldn't find jobs elsewhere. South Barrow is filled with people who used to be slaves, and they're still thinking like slaves. If we want to change that kind of place, then we want to have feelers on the council, because they make sure we're thinking clearly and that the people in South Barrow are thinking clearly. Their names will affect everything this council does."

Cale looked at the king. The king returned his stare and,

releasing a long sigh, gave a slight nod.

"Hamal," Cale said, turning back to him. "Of the vast library of names available to us, which names do you suggest we need specifically for the king's council as we seek to assist our brethren in the district of South Barrow?"

Hamal smiled. "You already know the answer to that question."

Cale paused. He blinked slowly. "I do?"

"Aye. You're the one who told me that there is no justice in South Barrow. Do you remember? That is what you told me just after I met you—you said there was no justice there. So we need to find a feeler named Justice and give him the job of making South Barrow better. If we do this, then there will be justice in South Barrow once more, and it will cause everything to start getting better."

"Hamal," Cale said. When he was seeing something, he always spoke slowly, and nearly a full minute passed before he continued his thought. The whole while, his gaze was sharp and strong—a true seer's gaze—as he looked at Hamal's face. "I do not believe a feeler named Justice was what I meant when I said that."

"But that is what you saw," Hamal replied. "You saw that justice needed to be there. A feeler named Justice would be the best and quickest way to make sure South Barrow has justice inside it. Then once we have Justice, we can find the other names we need, like Hope and Courage and Endurance. Names that will help us as we help our brothers and sisters in South Barrow."

Hamal looked around the table expectantly. Talking about the gifts always made him excited because he found them so fascinating. But he noticed no one else seemed quite as excited as he was.

He was still standing up when Lord Cecil Dersun, a reader, stood up also and began to talk about the importance of including on the king's council only those with adequate experience. Then Lord Jaron Madoran, a grower, stood up and questioned where they would ever be able to find a feeler with adequate experience when it came to the king's council.

It was like pulling a log out of a dam. When everyone started talking in loud voices, Hamal sat down quickly and wondered if this was why the king looked so tired after spending all day with his council. Who could get anything done when everyone wanted to talk in loud voices?

Then he noticed Cale and the king.

They were looking at each other across the table, neither one saying a word as the rest of the room fell to pieces. It was like they were speaking together, because the king would shrug from time to time with a strange little smile on his lips, and Cale's expression would change—the way it would in a natural conversation, one that Hamal could hear. What were they talking about?

The king finally looked at Hamal, who straightened in his chair. Cedrick nodded, but Hamal had the sense it was not a nod for him.

Cale held up his hand.

The room fell quiet. Conversations cut off. People sat down. Hamal blessed the silence.

"Your majesty," Cale said without bothering to rise. "I happen to know where we can find a feeler named Justice."

"Ah." The king's eyes glinted. "How convenient. And where would we find this master of government and great lord of wisdom?"

Hamal thought the king was teasing someone—maybe it was even him—but he couldn't quite tell.

"The west wing of the king's prison," Cale replied.

Whispers ran through the room. Just whispers this time, but they came with scowls.

Hamal knew the king's prison had two wings. One wing was where criminals like Masly Hawl lived in nice, spacious rooms with tables and chairs and real beds. That wing was nicer than most family dwellings found in South Barrow. But the other wing, the west wing, had not been fashioned to make men feel like men. It was dirty and smelled like rot and other things, and Hamal had heard stories about rats.

"Is the west wing the bad side?" Hamal whispered to Cale. Cale nodded. "Yes."

Hamal might not have much experience with king's councils, but he doubted they would want to put a criminal in charge of a city district, especially if that man had done something so wicked that he was still locked away in prison—and on the bad side, too. "What did a feeler named Justice do to get thrown in prison?"

Cale lifted his hand in a lazy sort of shrug and gave Hamal a half smile. "We will simply have to find out, won't we?"

Hamal grinned. "All right."

2 The Feeler Named Justice

The west wing of the prison smelled like everything terrible.

Hamal had been down here before—to visit Masly, but Masly lived in the prison's south wing, which was nicer and smelled clean and scrubbed, because it *was* clean and scrubbed. No one had scrubbed the west wing in a very, very long time.

Cale spoke quietly with the warden, and then he and Hamal waited in a little box of a room for the prisoner to be brought to them. Two small torches on the walls flickered with weak orange light in the darkness.

As the minutes passed, Hamal asked, "Why is Justice in prison?"

Cale didn't answer immediately. He looked around the room in a way that suggested he could see much more than the dirt on the walls and finally replied, "Perhaps a mistake was made."

"A mistake?"

"Yes. No legal system is flawless and mistakes sometimes occur. Granted, the justice gift itself allows us to come fairly close to perfection—those with the justice gift can perceive between innocence and guilt, no matter what the defendant is saying. But not every case is brought before them. Sometimes, depending on the defendant's crime and social status, magistrates decide his fate."

"What does that mean?" Hamal asked.

Cale focused on him. "Which part?"

"His crime and social status. Does that mean poor people go to prison more often?"

"No," Cale replied. "It means the king employs fifty justices, men and women with the gift, in his legal system, and they don't have time to hear every case. Therefore, they hire magistrates to work for them. Some of these magistrates are justices themselves, but most of the time, they're jewelers or growers, which means they occasionally make mistakes in their judgments. Each magistrate does his or her best work to determine whether or not the defendant is guilty."

"Oh." Hamal thought about what his friend was saying and tried to understand. "So you think Justice being here in prison might be a mistake?"

Cale shrugged. "If a feeler's name is as important as you say, would it be possible for a feeler named Justice to be unjust?"

"I think he would do what is right *most* of the time. How could he not? His name is his nature."

"His name is his nature," Cale repeated slowly. Humor flitted across his face. "I never know what gems I will hear from you, Hamal—or where I will hear them." He glanced through the room with distaste. "If his name is his nature, why do *you* think he is in prison?"

"I have no idea," Hamal replied.

Cale smiled. "We'll find out."

When the warden returned, he had two large guards with him, and Justice was shackled in between them. He was a big man who filled the room. Even though it was chilly here underground, his arms were bare, and in the torchlight Hamal saw that they were covered with tattoos. Were those birds? He thought maybe they were birds. He had never seen so many tattoos all on one body before. Justice had matted black hair that hung down his back and an equally dirty, matted beard. He also had only one eye—a patch concealed the left one. He wore heavy shackles on his wrists and ankles, with an iron chain linking them.

Cale stood from the bench. Justice towered over him by at least six inches, and the prisoner wasn't even standing up straight. He was huge.

In a voice that sounded completely calm, Cale asked, "Warden, what are the charges against this man?" He looked away from Justice and focused on the warden instead.

"Assault," the warden instantly replied. "History of violence. Nearly killed one of the city patrolmen. He's in here for another three years."

Justice said nothing about these charges, and Hamal, who was watching the man's face, didn't see any change upon it.

Turning back to the prisoner, Cale looked at him for a long time in silence. Hamal could tell his friend was seeing something, and it must have been something interesting, because it took Cale a long time to see all of it.

Cale said to the warden, "I would like a copy of his file. If you could leave it with your men outside the door, that would be our only requirement."

Hamal expected the warden to obey instantly. People tended to have that response around seers—they seemed almost nervous when a seer was in the room with them—but this man made no move to leave.

"Forgive me, my lord, but the prisoner is dangerous."

Cale looked at the warden, his eyes reflecting the pale torchlight. For a moment, they appeared more orange than silver. "I know what he is, Warden. You may go."

Concerned for their safety or not, none of the king's men had it in them to argue with a seer, especially not Cale, who was the king's right hand. The warden and his guards finally stepped out, closing the heavy wooden door behind them. Hamal, Cale, and the prisoner were left alone, and the room seemed still and quiet as if there were no people in it at all.

Justice stood in the middle of the space. The back of his head nearly brushed the ceiling. Hamal could hear the feeler's heartbeat, and it was steady and calm. For a man to be this calm in the midst of an examination—an examination by a seer, no less—Hamal thought it must be that Justice was a calm person. A man who didn't worry about things.

Cale looked at the prisoner for a long time. The moments passed, gathering up on top of one another, and when he'd seen whatever it was he'd intended to see, Cale sat down. He propped his left ankle on his opposite knee as if this were his private office and not a dirty room in a dirty prison, and he said, "Hamal, why don't you tell Justice why we are here?"

Hamal looked at him in surprise. And then, because he sometimes didn't understand other people's hints, he leaned toward Cale and asked hesitantly, "What do you want me to tell him?"

Cale looked remarkably relaxed for a man who had a "dangerous" prisoner standing right in front of him. He waved his hand. "Anything you wish."

"Anything?"

"Yes. Go ahead."

So Hamal stepped forward to look at the prisoner more closely. He liked most feelers, and he thought this was the first time he had met one named Justice. It was a good name, wasn't it? *Justice.* Justice was what a city needed; it was what South Barrow needed, and the name made him feel safe. They said that Justice was dangerous, yet Hamal was standing right in front of him in a small, confined space and he felt safe.

"What happened to your eye?" Hamal asked.

Justice looked down at him. A moment or two passed in silent assessment and then the man answered, "Lost it in a fight." He had a voice that matched his form. It was quiet but deep, almost more like a creature than a man. A big creature, one that knew how to protect all the smaller creatures. Hamal liked it.

"Did you really injure a city patrolman?"

"Yes."

"Why?"

The prisoner's one eye narrowed but not in an aggressive way. Instead, it was as if he found Hamal odd. "Because he deserved it." He said it simply, without malice, and it left no room for doubt. Justice had done what he felt necessary. They couldn't really expect anything else from a feeler named Justice, could they?

"What was the bad man doing?" Hamal asked.

Justice studied Hamal again. "Why do you think he was a bad man?"

Hamal replied with a smile, "I know it because your name is Justice, and you're a feeler. You wouldn't do something that you felt was unjust. You would have to feel it was just. It must be that you saw something that was wrong in South Barrow, and you decided to stop it, even though it meant attacking one of the king's men." As Hamal thought about it, he realized Justice was brave—braver, even, than Hamal had supposed a feeler named Justice would be. He had acted less like a typical feeler and more like a flamemaker or a weathermaker, who could be loud and passionate whenever they felt strongly about something. "You knew you would be arrested, didn't you? But you tried to stop the king's man anyway. He must have been doing something very bad. What was it?"

"You are the first person to ask me this," Justice said.

"But they would have—" Hamal frowned. "Didn't they ask you about it in the Court of Justice?"

"No."

Behind them on the bench, Cale sighed. Hamal heard the sound and knew what his friend was thinking. It didn't always happen this way, where he knew a seer's thoughts, but he could tell exactly what they were in this moment.

"Why not?" Hamal asked.

Justice shrugged. The shackles around his wrists jangled coldly. "You'll have to ask them. They asked me only one question, and it was how I pleaded. I told them yes, I had injured Krasak and they pronounced sentence."

"Who's Krasak?"

Justice's one eye peered down at him. "That is the patrolman who disagreed with my assessment of his actions."

Hamal nearly laughed and afterward didn't know why. There was something so very polite about the way Justice said those words, when the topic was quite serious. A man had nearly died because of him. The man had disagreed with Justice. Hamal thought that was an interesting way to think of it. "What was he doing that was bad?"

The feeler looked over at Cale sitting on the bench. The two men watched one another, and nothing seemed to be decided, for Justice turned back to Hamal. A long sigh escaped him, and Hamal thought Justice began to look relieved, like he had been waiting a long time for the opportunity to say these things. Adjusting his weight in his dirty boots, the feeler said, "They curse the king in South Barrow. They consider him as unjust as a tyrant."

Hamal gasped and didn't realize he had done so until the

sound was out in the open. Those words were familiar to him. *Cursing the king.* He had heard words just like them many, many times. He felt Cale's gaze brush across him, as strong as if the seer had said his name, and Hamal asked Justice in a whisper, "Why do they curse the king in South Barrow?"

"They blame him for their poverty. Landan was the one who freed them from slavery, but somehow in their view, he took away their homes and livelihoods. It is as if they believe he made them slaves, instead of setting them free. They blame Landan for their current lack. But Cedrick, his son, is the one they curse, blaming him for their oppression. There's a saying in South Barrow that the king takes no prisoners. They believe him to be a tyrant because those he arrests are never seen again."

Hamal knew this story from his time in South Barrow. He knew it and he hated it.

"They have an opinion of the king that is vastly untrue," Justice continued, "and it took me some time to discover why they held to it so severely. One of the house lords was paying Krasak to 'arrest' the poor in the king's name and ship them as prisoners out of the city. This has been going on for two years, long enough to condition the people to blame and hatred. Krasak was…" Justice stopped, his gaze on Hamal's face. "What is it?"

Hamal realized he was frowning. He looked over at Cale, who had risen off the bench and was staring at Justice in an odd way. "Druis Ephram, Cale. Isn't that the lord's name?"

Justice blinked, and for the first time, Hamal heard the feeler's heart stumble in its steps. Justice was the one who answered the question, not Cale. "Yes. That's the one. That's him." Air scraped his throat and he added, "It took me five months to discover the name you speak so easily now. How do you know it, sir?"

Cale did not sit down again. Hamal glanced at him, waiting for his friend to speak.

"Druis Ephram," Cale said at last, "was arrested six weeks ago on multiple counts of kidnapping and endangerment. He has agreed to the king's terms, and his son is in the process of shutting down the mine that was illegally receiving our people. He is returning the stolen to their families and paying them decent wages for their time, plus compensation. The story was completed in your absence." Cale added, "We are ensuring the delivery of justice in this matter, as much as we can."

Justice's eye closed. His breath rolled out of him quietly.

Cale waited to speak again until Justice was looking at him. "We've known about Druis Ephram for six weeks. Hamal, in fact, was the one who told us about the arrests in the first place." Cale motioned to Hamal, but he kept his gaze on Justice as if trying to pry the man open with his eyes alone. It was a look only a seer could give. "But here is the question. You were arrested four months ago—why did we have to wait for Hamal to tell us what was occurring in South Barrow? Why did you not tell us yourself?"

Justice frowned at Cale, and for a moment, his gaze was as intense as Cale's could be. "You are correct, my lord. That is the question." The muscles flexed in his throat before, finally, his tension seemed to pass. When he spoke next, he did so calmly, with passion but also with a noticeable lack of anger. "Why did you have to wait for Hamal? Why did no one see the injustice years ago, when it first began? How is it possible that it has been going on this long, and no one noticed?"

The small room dropped into quiet. Cale said nothing and Hamal waited. He knew Cale well enough by this point to know the man would not leave the question unanswered. Cale did not leave anything unanswered, if he could help it.

Cale ran his hand over his face—a movement Hamal saw but rarely with him—and scowled as he looked over at the door.

His gaze grew sharp, and Hamal wondered what his friend was seeing and why a door would be of such interest. What was this conversation truly about? Hamal couldn't quite tell anymore. He felt like he had missed a few key points and wished for Cale to explain them to him.

Cale motioned with his hand, like he was giving a signal to continue, and Hamal didn't understand at first. *Continue? Continue what?* But then he remembered. *Oh, yes.* They had come here for a reason. They had come on behalf of the king.

"Do you want a job?" Hamal asked, tilting his head back to meet Justice's gaze. "You'll need to be on your best behavior and not beat up anyone, but it's a good job with good pay. And it smells much better than this place. Are you interested?"

Justice didn't look surprised, and his heart didn't skip again, but he did glance at Cale before replying, "What's the job?"

Cale laughed deep in his throat. The unexpected sound drew all eyes to him. "Oh," he said with a dark sort of amusement, "we're going to give you South Barrow."

3 The Man Who Wasn't from South Barrow

Though the warden strongly protested, Cale had a written order from the king that released Justice Hewen into his custody. Hamal didn't understand the particulars, but apparently that piece of paper somehow meant that Justice was now Cale's prisoner, instead of the warden's. So in the end, it didn't matter if the warden thought the prisoner was dangerous. It also didn't matter that a dozen guards with scowls and narrowed eyes escorted Hamal, Cale, and Justice out of the prison to the waiting coach.

When Cale saw Justice's face in the early afternoon sunlight, he stopped still and turned to look at him more closely. This halted the whole procession, and Hamal, wondering what had made Cale upset, ran into Justice from behind. His arm brushed the feeler's waist, and he took a quick, startled breath and didn't need to look at the man's face to know what Cale had seen.

Cale turned to the warden. "If I ever hear even the rumor of this happening within your administration again, I will have you shipped to Southpost as a latrine steward." That was all he said, but the words were stated with an eerie sort of calm that drew all the color out of the warden's face.

"The prisoner is violent," the warden tried to say.

"A simple 'yes' will suffice," Cale said, the words quiet.

"Yes, Commander."

"What will you do differently in the future?"

"I will take much greater pains to ensure that none of the prisoners are mishandled. Some of my men can be overly zealous to keep the peace—sir."

"I would not ship your men to Southpost, Warden. I would just ship you."

"They will learn, sir. They will."

Once in the coach, Justice filled up one whole bench by himself. Looking out the window, he sat there and absently rubbed his wrists where the shackles had been. He was twenty-three years old, which his bones had told Hamal in that brief encounter on the walkway, and none of his bones were familiar with bitterness. It was an interesting thing, Hamal thought, to meet a man who—perhaps—should have had a different sentence, who clearly had seen much injustice during that sentence, and yet there was not a single quill stroke of bitterness anywhere inside him. Instead, Hamal took note that the feeler's bones were accustomed to waiting. That was what they said more than anything else—this was a man who was patient.

Justice stared out the window as if he'd never seen the city before, and Hamal thought about how the man had just spent four months in complete darkness.

Sliding forward on the bench, Hamal asked, "Justice?"

The large man looked at him.

"May I see your hand, please?"

Without hesitation, Justice held out his hand. Hamal took it with both of his own—the man's hands were twice the size of Hamal's—and set about repairing his bruises and fixing six ribs that had healed on their own without a healer's care. He had been beaten maybe five times in the last four months, but most of his injuries were internal, which was good. Hamal was quite talented at fixing bones, but skin gave him some trouble. He tended to leave scars.

"Thank you," the feeler said when Hamal was finished. Then his head tilted and he asked, "Are you the same Hamal who used to live in South Barrow?"

Hamal looked at Justice in surprise. "Yes! Do you know me?"

There was movement behind Justice's thick beard, and Hamal thought it might have been a small smile. "I've heard of you. The feeler clan in South Barrow told me several stories about the boy healer who lived with the flamemakers. Do you remember a feeler named Bravery?"

"No, I don't think so. How did I know him?"

"You found him in Baker's Alley, just after thieves had attacked him and left him for dead, but you somehow managed to drag him back into life."

"How did he die?"

The muscles tightened in Justice's jaw, but his answer was calm. "They cut his throat."

"Oh, yes!" Hamal exclaimed. "I do remember him! How is he? How is his wife? He was going home to his wife, and he didn't want her to worry."

"Both were doing well the last time I saw them. He's a good friend of mine. You saved the life of my friend." Justice nodded slowly. "I appreciate this."

He said nothing more for the rest of the drive.

They took him to Cale's house on Merchant Street. When Justice climbed from the coach and stretched with his tattooed arms over his head, he seemed bigger than ever. Now that he stood upright, he was taller than Cale by more than a full head, and Cale was not a short man. Perhaps this was one reason the warden's guards had responded to Justice with such violence. Maybe they had been a little afraid of him. The feeler hadn't had any trouble injuring that one fellow—what was his name again? *Oh, yes. It's Krasak*—and he probably wouldn't have had any trouble injuring his jailors either.

Inside the house, Cale turned Justice over to his steward and requested that the feeler join them for dinner in three hours. He did not seem alarmed in the slightest to have Justice in his home, even though Satha, his wife, had returned with them from Brannack, and she was somewhere in the house as well. Hamal liked that Cale seemed to think about Justice the same way Hamal thought about him.

"There is something calming about him, isn't there?" Hamal said. "Justice makes me feel calm. But do you think it was odd that he didn't make the warden feel that way?"

Cale waited until Justice had gone up the steps with the steward before answering. "Justice is…different than I was expecting, yes. Tell me what you know of him. You had your hands on him for several minutes in the coach; what did his bones and blood tell you?"

"Well," Hamal began, "he's younger than you, just twenty-three. No brothers or sisters. His father died when he was very young, but his mother is still alive, and she's married now to someone Justice deeply respects. He loves him, I think. He misses them both, and he hasn't seen them in quite some time."

Cale's brows began a slow walk up his forehead. "You can see so much about his family, just by listening to his body?"

Hamal shrugged. "Justice's blood likes to talk. He himself might be quiet, but his blood is not. I don't think Justice is a man who likes to hide things from people, and his blood is much the same way."

Cale lifted one finger. "Ah. An interesting point to make about a feeler named Justice. Remember that point, Hamal—that Justice does not hide—but please continue with your report. What else do you know about him?"

"Well, I know that all his tattoos were done on the same day, which sounds like a dreadful experience, and he lost his eye when he was eleven. I'm not exactly sure what happened, but I think it involved a tree out in the woods. He fell on something. He told us he lost the eye in a fight, and I think that fight wasn't with a person. There are some interesting scrapes in his eye socket, little nicks in the bone—"

Hamal started laughing when he saw Cale's expression. There were times when he forgot that the other gifts didn't always appreciate a healer's details. Cale, perhaps more than some, did not enjoy hearing about injuries to eyes.

"The king will ask us about the eye," Cale said, clearing his throat. "And he will be relieved to hear we were not in any way responsible for its loss."

Hamal shook his head. "Justice was eleven. The eye happened many, many years before he was arrested."

"Did you notice anything particular when he was speaking to us today?"

"What do you mean?"

"I mean that he told us his story without giving us many details about himself at all. His tale was almost *diplomatic* in its level of concealment. We know why he was arrested, but we don't know what he was doing in South Barrow in the first place."

Hamal felt himself frown. "Isn't he from South Barrow?"

Silver light twinkled in Cale's eyes. "He isn't from South Barrow any more than you are."

"I was just living there for a while because I hadn't found anywhere else to live."

Cale nodded. "Justice's situation is a bit different than yours. He *chose* to live in South Barrow. He had a reason for doing so, though I cannot see what that reason is at this moment. I do know, however, that he is originally from Port Morden. From the Governor's District, to be specific, which is one of the wealthier districts in that city. He may have been a guard there, or a high-level servant, but whatever he was, he is used to much finer things than what he found in South Barrow."

Cale drew Hamal's attention to the file the warden had given them. Justice's file. Tapping it with his finger, he said, "According to his file, another feeler was arrested with him—a man named Steadfast, who is noted here as Justice's servant. When you were living in South Barrow, did you meet a single person who employed a servant?"

"A servant in South Barrow?" Hamal shook his head. "Never. No one could afford servants in South Barrow. They wanted to *be* servants. They wanted to be anything, so they could feed their families. That's why we've been going there and trying to help them."

"Yet Justice had a servant. What does that tell you?"

Hamal thought about it. "He has money?"

Cale agreed. "Exactly. He had a reason for living in South Barrow, and that reason had nothing to do with lack, as it does for every other resident. As it did for you. Why would a man with some amount of wealth at his disposal choose to live in poverty?"

Hamal looked at the steps Justice and Cale's steward had ascended a few minutes ago. He couldn't help but notice how clean the steps were; everything in Cale's fine, expensive house was clean—except for Justice Hewen. The steward had looked at Justice with horror in his eyes and hurried him away, calling for additional servants to come and help him. Justice, meanwhile, had rubbed at his bearded jaw like he was trying to stifle a laugh.

"Maybe he was trying to help people," Hamal suggested.

"Perhaps."

Hamal turned to his friend in surprise. "Perhaps? Only perhaps?"

Cale frowned. "I don't doubt his desire to help others. I am of a mind to think well of Justice, just as you do. I can see his honesty. In fact, I can see it in him more than I can see it in certain others. In some ways, he is easier to read than others. However, it also seems that he is purposefully keeping a secret, and before he steps into an important position serving the king, we will need to discover what that secret is. Hamal, I believe it is time for us to consult the oracle."

"I thought she didn't like it when you called her that."

Cale smiled. "Someday, when you marry, you will understand why I do."

There were times when Hamal's friend Cale was quite strange.

4 The Letters The Seer Found Interesting

They found Cale's wife in the upstairs sitting room. Every time Hamal stepped through the doorway, he always thought the room was rather pretty. The walls were pale blue with little flowers painted on them, and gauzy white curtains hung across the large windows. Everything seemed quiet and peaceful and airy and bright, which was why Satha had chosen this room to be her workshop. She currently sat on a tall stool in front of a canvas much bigger than she was, and she peered at them around the edge as they entered the room.

Hamal smiled when he saw the blue slash of paint on her nose. She was quite fond of telling him that she had no idea what she was doing with paints, but she enjoyed them all the same. For a week or so after he had healed her, she'd tripped over steps and the corners of rugs, dropped food in her lap, and knocked her teacup hard against her teeth. She had to learn how to move with sight, instead of just weight and sound and sense, and now she was learning how to use a paintbrush. He supposed that in the years of an artist, she was probably about three.

She looked at Cale with sharp silver eyes. "Who is that large, dirty man with the beard and the tattoos that you have let into our house like an old family friend?"

Hamal grinned. He liked living with two seers. You never knew what they would say next. It was like a game, one that lasted all day long and made you laugh. "He's a feeler! And don't worry—he won't be dirty for long. It's just that we pulled him out of prison."

"Hmm," Satha replied, eyeing her husband. "How very nice."

Cale stepped up to one side of her canvas and ventured no farther. He would tease her and call her an oracle—a kind of seer who could see into the realm of the gods—but there he would stop. He had learned not to view her paintings until she was ready to reveal them. "What have you seen?"

"A large and dirty man."

"Yes, you said that."

Her eyes narrowed. "And what, husband of mine, causes you to believe I have seen anything more?"

"Experience," Cale replied.

She smiled, pleased, and straightened on the stool, disappearing behind the canvas. A moment passed, and then her voice floated out to them. "He's a feeler. He was born in northern King's Barrow, somewhere up near the coast, where you can see the sea from almost any window in the house. As a child, he spent a great deal of time in the North Woods. He loves horses but not snakes. He loves the water and sand but does not like swimming. He was recently a student at a university, and the name of his house is not what he says it is."

Her head reappeared around the canvas, and she looked at her husband with such expectancy that Hamal wanted to laugh and kiss the blue paint on her nose.

Cale nodded. "Well done. I saw similarly, in all cases but one. The name of his house. He says it is *Hewen*. You disagree?"

She shook her head. A piece of dark hair slid out of the red ribbon she was using as a tie. "I can't tell you that I disagree. It's possible that *is* his name—a family name of some sort—but it is not the name he is known by. I mean to say, he has not told the full truth concerning his name." She paused. "Did you invite him to dinner?"

"I did."

"You invited a prisoner to dinner."

"Former prisoner."

"I'm sure his crime was something calm and serene, yes? Like jewel theft. Or snatching a painting."

"Assault, actually."

She sniffed. "Of course." Wrinkling her nose at her husband, she disappeared behind the canvas.

Hamal covered his mouth with both hands to hide his laughter.

"He'll be on his best behavior," her husband called to her. "Hamal told him he had to be, and I'm sure he was listening."

Cale was busy the rest of the afternoon. He sent one man into South Barrow to make subtle inquiries about the patrolman named Krasak and another man to Rannis Hadley, captain of city patrol. Then he sat down at his desk with Justice's file.

"Justice Hewen," Cale told Hamal, "or whatever his real name may be, seems to be a man of strength and passion. Would you not agree?"

Sitting on the couch, Hamal nodded and wondered what the seer was thinking.

"He claims," Cale went on, "to have known about Druis Ephram's betrayal of the king weeks before we did. I believe him in this matter. Yet…why is it that he sat in prison for four months and did not say a word about it? Assault of a city patrolman is taken very seriously, so I understand how it happened that the magistrate—Jere Derhart, his name is—did not give Justice the opportunity to speak in court. Granted, he should have been given the opportunity, but I understand why the magistrate believed the matter self-explanatory. Justice calmly admits doing exactly what they claimed he did. But why do you suppose Justice made no effort to stop Krasak from prison?"

Cale looked up from the file. "According to his file, he did not write a single letter during his imprisonment. He fought with his guards whenever he had the opportunity and was difficult to manage the entire time, from his arrest up until yesterday—when, I imagine, he obtained that deep bruise across his forehead, which you healed. His file clearly states that he made no requests to see anyone. No friends or family."

"But his servant," Hamal interjected. "You said he had a servant with him. He would be concerned about his servant."

"Yes, I agree—he would certainly be concerned, especially if he felt something untoward was happening. It is possible he thought the servant was in danger. Yet according to his file, Justice made no effort to follow up with him. Neither did the servant attempt to see Justice in prison." Cale nodded slowly, a frown building in his expression. "That, of course, means this is all quite unfortunate, Hamal."

"About the servant, you mean?"

"No. The fact that what I see concerning Justice and what I read in his file are two different things." With a sigh, Cale leaned back in his chair. "I find it difficult to believe that your feeler named Justice would stay silent when others demand it of him. He does not seem like a man who shivers and quakes when pressure is applied. It is one thing for a magistrate to assume he has all the facts and, therefore, to mishandle a case. But it is quite another for a man's guards, by their own volition, to refuse to allow that man to have a voice. Unfortunately, it is beginning to seem to me that Justice has not seen much of his name."

"What are we going to do?" Hamal asked.

Cale's mouth twitched, and a glint of humor appeared in his knowing silver gaze. "I believe we officially have a case. Let's go into South Barrow tonight, meet up with my man there, and see what we can discover."

Before Hamal could answer, there was a knock on the door and Kerwin, Cale's steward, entered the room, something square and papery in his hand. He was a slight man not much taller than Hamal and a weathermaker who seemed to favor calm skies. Hamal had never seen him upset or even out of sorts with any of those on his staff.

"Forgive the intrusion, my lord," Kerwin said, coming all the way into the room. He shut the door discreetly behind him. "But I thought you might wish to see this. Your guest asked for writing supplies before I could persuade him to do anything else. He completed two letters in short order and asked for them to be given to the local courier."

Kerwin set the letters in Cale's hand. Hamal slid off the couch and went to see what the steward found so interesting.

The first envelope was addressed to Corin Groff of Newbold Street.

"Who is that?" Hamal asked in a whisper, because when you were looking at someone else's letters, it seemed like a good idea to whisper.

"I don't know," Cale answered absently and tapped an edge of the envelope with one finger. After a moment, he added something he had seen about the house. "It's a secondary house, this building on Newbold Street. No one lives there unless they are in town, which I don't believe they are. So Justice is sending a letter to a house that is likely empty. That is interesting by itself."

The second envelope was addressed to Norris Orissar of the

palace.

"Wait—I know that name," Hamal exclaimed. "Don't I?"

Cale blinked once, did so again, and then looked up at Kerwin. Kerwin nodded, a serious expression on his face, and said, "That, my lord, is why I thought you might want to see what he was doing."

"Who is Norris Orissar?" Hamal asked and noticed it was entertaining to say those two words close together. *Norris Orissar. Norris Orissar.*

"He is the king's secretary," Cale murmured, turning the letters over in his hands. In a pensive tone he asked, "Why would Justice write the king?"

"I have no idea. Do you see anything important?"

Cale looked sideways at Hamal, brows rising. "You expect me to spy on the contents of another man's letters?"

Hamal laughed. "No. I expect you to be a seer and know things."

Cale grunted and held the letters up, one in each hand, as if he meant to show the ceiling the addresses written upon the envelopes. He stared at them both and then lowered the one on the right, the one addressed to Corin Groff. "Justice knows the residents of the house on Newbold Street. He was staying there before he moved into South Barrow."

The letter addressed to the king's secretary stayed right where it was for nearly a full minute. Then it lowered, too. "He writes to make an appointment with the king." Cale looked at Hamal oddly and then turned to Kerwin. "Has he said anything noteworthy to you?"

The steward shook his head. "No, my lord. He has not said much of anything, to anyone."

"Is it so strange that one of the king's subjects would write a letter to him?" Hamal asked.

"No," Cale returned. "The interesting thing is that Justice fully expects to be granted his request."

5 The Weathermaker Who Died

That evening, Rannis Hadley, captain of city patrol, appeared on Cale's doorstep half an hour before dinner. Hamal startled when he saw the large man walk into the front entry. He had never seen the captain outside of patrol headquarters or a darkened alley where some horrible event had occurred. It seemed the man had come straight from his office because he had a deep line between his brows and a large stain on his tunic like someone had spilled a cup of tea on him.

"Hamal," Captain Hadley growled in greeting.

"Hello, Captain! What are you doing here?"

Cale stepped into the entry from the hallway, and Hadley looked over at him, holding aloft a plain brown file. "I am delivering something, like a common servant. You wanted my file on Justice Hewen? Well, here it is. Delivered personally, as you can see. And yes, there's a reason."

Cale's steps slowed and then stopped. His eyes took on that intense seer cast as he looked at the captain, and Hadley started muttering something about seers and time and how he didn't care what anyone thought.

"Come into the sitting room," Cale invited.

The three of them walked down the hall into the sitting room, which had blue walls and windows that faced the southern garden. This was the same room where, just a few weeks ago, Hamal had healed Satha's eyes—in that chair right over there, the one with the roses stitched into the fabric. Hamal was particularly fond of this room.

A servant closed the door behind them.

Cale turned to the captain. "Tell me."

"I've had a long, trying day," the captain replied.

Hamal had no idea why the captain felt that was important to say, but Cale seemed to understand. Walking to the door, the seer called to a servant, who returned a short time later with a tea tray. Cale himself poured the captain a cup of tea, added honey and cream, and handed the teacup to him in exchange for Justice's file. Hadley sank onto the middle of the couch with a rough sigh as Cale sat in Satha's chair and opened the file. Watching them both, Hamal perched on the arm of the couch and folded his hands in his lap.

Cale spoke first. His gaze on the file, he said, "I requested only a copy of Justice Hewen's file. What in this file interests you to the extent that you have come yourself?"

Hadley sipped his tea. "On the contrary, Justice Hewen is not of interest to me. Krasak is one of my men, and you released his assailant. I would like to know why."

Cale waved his hand toward the couch arm where Hamal was sitting. "Hamal, tell him why."

Hamal shifted as Hadley's dark eyes found him. The captain's gaze could almost feel like Cale's sometimes, especially when the captain wasn't satisfied with something. There was weight behind it. The weight of an entire city. Hamal decided it would be good if he started his explanation at the very beginning. "Do you have any feelers who work for you?"

"Yes."

Hamal straightened up, blinking at him. Then he grinned. "You do? Oh, good! What do they do for you?"

Hadley sipped from the teacup, and across the top of it, he studied Hamal with a frown. "They assist with interrogations."

"Oh, I imagine they would be quite good at that—at helping you know what a suspect is feeling. You could probably solve a good many cases working with feelers, couldn't you?

Hadley grunted. "Their assistance has proven helpful from time to time—provided the feeler doesn't run out of the room weeping. That happens, too. What does this have to do with Justice Hewen?"

"Well, he's a feeler."

The line between the captain's brows began to twitch. He glanced at Cale, heaved another sigh, and said, "I am aware of this, Hamal."

"Have you ever noticed how certain feelers can handle certain cases better than others?"

Hadley shifted the teacup in his hands, fiddling with it. "Explain."

"Out of the feelers who work for you, what is the name of the feeler you like the best?"

Hadley hesitated before rumbling, "His name is Temperance."

Hamal looked over at Cale. "What does *temperance* mean?"

"Restraint," the seer supplied. "Self-control."

"Well, no wonder you like him the best! He probably is calm and peaceful, isn't he? A feeler's name is very important. They are strong in whatever they are named. Temperance is good at keeping himself under control, so you appreciate him. Justice Hewen is good at knowing what is right and what is wrong."

Hadley fixed Hamal with a heavy stare. "Justice Hewen," he said and made a face, "broke both of Krasak's arms, shattered his jaw, and snapped four of his ribs. Does it sound like he was *right* in this instance?"

Hamal felt himself flush. He adjusted his position on the couch's arm so he wouldn't accidentally fall off the side and answered as calmly as he could. "I don't know what to say. But I would trust Justice's version of the story more than I would trust Krasak's version."

"Because Justice knows the difference between right and wrong?"

"Aye."

Hadley leaned forward. "Then what does that say about Krasak?"

"Well, I think it means there must be a reason Justice did what he did."

Hadley frowned at Hamal a moment longer. Then he blew out his breath, and with it the fire seemed to roll out of him. He settled back onto the couch and did something unexpected— he gave Hamal a rare smile that nearly accomplished what his intensity had not. Hamal caught himself just before sliding off the couch.

"I have found," the captain said grandly, "that a man's story sometimes changes when it is presented from a different perspective. Justice pounded the blood from my patrolman. He has never denied this, and it is a highly punishable offense." He looked over at Cale. "However…"

Cale had observed this exchange with a cool silver gaze, the file still open but now ignored in his hands. "You," he said to Hadley, "know something about Krasak. You are wondering if Justice Hewen might have been justified in his response."

"No," Hadley replied and set his empty teacup on the table. "Based on my understanding of the case, I would not say that Justice Hewen's actions were justified." He paused. "But if you can *prove* they were justified, I would appreciate it. Krasak is a jeweler, one of the few jewelers who work for me. I don't hire many jewelers because they usually don't stay long. They rush off to larger and more expensive ventures. But Krasak has seemed content to work for me for the past three years. He asked to be stationed in South Barrow, and I thought it was because he enjoyed the challenge. I have to put a certain kind of man in South Barrow—it isn't work that appeals to everyone."

"What happened to cause you to question Krasak?" Cale asked.

Hadley looked down at his teacup before answering, "Krasak's partner died last week. A weathermaker. He was on leave in Riverstone and died of heart failure. At thirty-one."

"Surprisingly young," Cale murmured.

"Yes. He was in excellent physical condition, too; he had been examined by a healer the week before after an altercation in East Barrow. A hopeful thief had clouted him across the head and shoved him into the river, but Ledaran managed to climb out on his own. A city healer pronounced him perfectly fit."

"A healer said he was healthy, but then he died a few days later from heart failure?" Hamal asked. "That doesn't make any sense."

"No, it doesn't. However, as unusual as the death was, I might have overlooked it. I have eight open cases on my desk right now that involve deaths much more suspicious than heart failure. But I didn't overlook it." Hadley turned on the couch and looked at Hamal pointedly. "And it's because of a feeler."

"A feeler who works for you?"

"Yes. She was in the room when Krasak heard the news about his partner, and she reported that he was not surprised. He was saddened by the death of his partner, but there was no shock within him, no surprise at all. I don't tend to take feelers and their suppositions seriously—she's a maintenance worker, not a patrolman, an investigator, or anything similar—but she came to see me and raised a valid point. If he was not surprised, it *does* suggest that he knew about his partner's death before it occurred."

"What does that mean?" Hamal asked, looking back and forth between Cale and the captain.

For a moment, the sitting room was quiet.

"It could mean a variety of things," Hadley answered. "Could also mean I delivered the file personally so I could make a request."

He wanted something? And it had something to do with Krasak? Hamal watched the captain and waited.

"You want us to look at the body," Cale said.

Hadley stood up off the couch. He was a tall man, and Hamal wondered what it would feel like to be squeezed into the same room with Captain Hadley *and* Justice Hewen.

"I simply wish to verify how Ledaran died," Hadley stated. "If it truly was heart failure like my staff healer declared, very well. If it was anything else, I want to know about it. When you sent your man for Justice Hewen's file, I realized you might have an indirect interest in Ledaran's case. He's buried in Grower's Park, in East Barrow. We can be there in an hour. My men are disturbing his eternal rest as we speak, and they will be ready for us by the time we arrive."

"Fine," Cale agreed. "But I have a request. There will be an addition to our party."

Hadley muttered something Hamal couldn't make out, and then he said, "I don't see what good it will do, but if that's what you want. You're the seer."

"What addition?" Hamal asked.

From Satha's chair Cale looked over at Hamal. His brows lifted as he stated, "Justice will be going with us."

6 Hamal's Grand Experiment

When Justice walked into the entry a few minutes later, Cale stopped talking and Captain Hadley straightened up as if his tutor had just reprimanded him.

Hamal grinned. He had known exactly what Justice looked like under all the grime, the matted hair, and the bruising; he'd put his hands on the feeler and healed him, so he knew all about his bones and his skin and the way his face was shaped. But knowing it with his gift was a little different than seeing it walk into the room.

Kerwin the steward had done a marvelous job with Justice Hewen. The beard was gone; the hair had been treated like an overgrown hedgerow and chopped back, and somewhere they had managed to find Justice clothes that actually fit him. All the slime and grunge and prison life had been scrubbed away, and Hamal was looking at a completely new man who seemed remarkably comfortable in a wealthy house. In fact, it seemed to Hamal that Justice would be at home even in the king's palace. That was Hamal's first thought—that Justice was used to palaces.

"Why, Justice!" Hamal exclaimed. "You look different."

Justice smiled. Hamal could tell it was a smile this time, now that the beard was gone. The feeler didn't seem to be a man who smiled grandly, the way some men did, but the smile filled his eyes and gave him warmth and seemed genuine. It was something to be enjoyed because it was special and rare.

"It was much needed," the feeler agreed.

Justice's gaze focused on Cale briefly and then turned to Captain Hadley, and Hamal introduced them. "This is Captain Hadley. He's in charge of city patrol. Oh, he's also the man Krasak works for."

Cale looked at Hamal sharply. But before the seer could say anything one way or another, Justice stepped forward and held out his hand to Hadley, who took it after a moment's hesitation. Justice was taller than the captain, and a little slimmer, and Hamal had the swift impression that Hadley was not used to looking up to anyone.

"A pleasure to meet you, sir," Justice said. "Whenever I hear your name, it is said with honor, even among those who, by their own designs, would feel they had a reason to dishonor it. You are doing fine work in the city, particularly in South Barrow."

Reclaiming his hand, Hadley didn't say a word at first, and then he spoke only after a good deal of throat clearing. "Justice Hewen, is it?"

"Indeed."

"I understand you have some...questions about your sentence." Hadley looked at Justice with narrowed eyes.

Justice shook his head. "No, sir. Not at all. My sentence is just."

Hadley cleared his throat again and looked over at Cale, and for the first time since Hamal had met him, the captain seemed to lack for words.

Hamal stepped up to Justice and tapped his tattooed arm. When the large man looked down at him, Hamal said, "We're going to go look at a body. Would you like to come?"

"Whose body?"

"A patrolman who died last week. A man named Ledaran."
Hamal was watching, and he didn't see any signs of recognition
in Justice's eyes. It seemed that Justice did not know Ledaran the
same way he knew Krasak.

"And what good will it be to have me there, Hamal? I am a
feeler—I couldn't tell you anything about a body."

Hamal grinned. "You can help me confirm the cause of
death."

"How would he do such a thing?" Cale asked.

"And how would I do that?" Justice asked at the same time
and seemed surprised that Cale had spoken, too.

Hamal laughed at their faces. He truly enjoyed it when Cale
looked at him this way, as if Hamal were the strangest person
ever to walk the earth. It was quite nice. This was one reason the
two of them made such fine friends. "We'll do an experiment! I
already have one in mind. We'll try it and see what happens."

Grower's Park was a quiet, secluded hill that overlooked
King's River. Some of the oldest tombs on the continent were
here, protecting the bodies of the ancient Dasken kings. Hamal
hadn't been to this hill in many years, and it looked different
than he remembered. The trees had changed. There were more
of them—and in different places. And the hill was no longer a
garden filled with flowers and trails and pleasant places to sit.
Now it was filled with the dead. The kings were buried at the top
of the hill, where the view was the best. Then came the family
tombs of the noble houses, followed by the plain gravesites of
commoners like Hamal. Like Cale and his family. But not like
Satha, Cale's wife. She, from the king's house, would be buried
where she could see the river in all its splendor.

The coach pulled to a stop in a little glen near the base of the hill.

In the moment or two before Captain Hadley started growling directions, Cale turned and faced the incline, looking up toward the crest where the kings were buried. Hamal followed his look but couldn't see anything but trees and a few memory houses made of marble and gold. The tombs of the noble families.

"This place always makes me think of Morden," Cale said quietly. In the evening sunlight, his eyes appeared orange. "I think of the adventure that was King's Barrow in those years, when the nation was young. All historians agree that Morden was a great man."

The first king of King's Barrow. The man who refused to fight his brothers for the Dasken throne, so he separated his kingdom into two pieces, giving his brothers their choice of land. They chose the southern portion, which was the wealthiest at the time, so King Morden came here, where his ancestors were buried on this hill. Now Morden was up there somewhere, too. He had died years and years ago, when Hamal was just a child.

"Oh, not me," Hamal said and Cale glanced at him. "This place doesn't make me think of Morden. I think of Morden when I visit my grandfather. They were good friends, you know. My grandfather says he would have done anything Morden told him to do, because Morden was wise."

Cale blinked at him. "That is a compliment indeed. Shel Galen, your grandfather, was instrumental in the formation of King's Barrow. We have multiple records of his famous declaration of King's Barrow in her infancy—that we are a country built on wisdom. We are the only nation on the earth founded by a sage."

Hamal lifted one shoulder in a shrug.

Cale stared at him. "What is it?"

"Yes, he said that, but he didn't say it because *he* was wise. He said it because of Morden. Morden was wise. And my grandfather loved him dearly. He wrote many books about him, you know. There are more books written about Morden and King's Barrow than have ever been written about Theraine or Dasken or any other place. And it is because my grandfather loved his friend. With Morden he found he had much to say. Some of his books are simply interviews with him. Shel would ask questions and write down whatever Morden said."

Justice joined them. "Shel Galen is your grandfather?" he rumbled in his deep voice.

Hamal looked up at him. "Yes, he is. He is a reader and he is very wise."

"That is the name of your house? Galen?"

"Yes." Hamal wondered why the feeler was interested. Until this moment, only Cale had asked him about his house name. It was as if everyone else assumed he didn't have one. "It's a very old name, and I don't use it often. Why would I? I'm not a reader like my grandfather." He laughed. "My name isn't written on the covers of thousands of books. I am just a healer."

Justice's brows rose slowly up his forehead. "Indeed. *Just* a healer." His tone was strange, though he spoke calmly. "You're a sage."

"I prefer the word *healer*. People aren't confused when I tell them I'm just a healer. If I tell them I'm a sage, I have to explain things."

"Hamal Galen, sage," Cale murmured.

Justice nodded as if he and Cale understood one another, and they didn't say anything else.

Captain Hadley stepped around the coach. "This way, gentlemen," he said, and they followed him and his men down a narrow footpath through the trees.

This area of the park reminded Hamal of the king's garden, located in the palace's center courtyard. Flamemakers kept it warm all year round, and the king, a grower and a direct descendent of Morden, tended his garden most faithfully. From time to time, Cale met the king there in the quiet, and he always seemed relaxed afterward. Grower's Park was a large area—an entire hill—and it was not heated all year round, and the trees showed the early signs of spring. There had been heavy snow just a few weeks ago, but that was all forgotten now, and Hamal heard birds singing from the bare branches. It was warmer today than it had been. He had barely remembered to bring his coat with him, and for Hamal, that meant a great deal.

They walked past dozens of gravestones. Some of them were covered with flowers and thick ivy that was already green and looked as old as the stones themselves. These were the graves of growers, whose descendants remembered them.

At the end of the path they reached the rest of Hadley's men. The earth had been disturbed; there were dirty shovels lying nearby. Four men waited near a new casket sitting just off the path. Cale didn't hesitate when he saw it, but Hamal felt a sudden emptiness behind him and turned to see Justice hanging back, a greenish hue on his face.

"Is something the matter, Justice?"

"I don't do well in graveyards," the feeler replied.

Hamal supposed that was true. Rubbing his scalp with one hand, he wondered what a feeler felt in an area of land where people had wept and prayed and felt heartbroken, and this had been going on for centuries. There were some very old graves here. The land knew old tears, and feelers had a sense about such things. They were almost like charters in that respect.

Hamal walked back to the feeler and took his arm. "I know," he told him gently, drawing the large man forward. "But we don't have to stay for long. Do you remember what Cale said in the coach? Ledaran might have been murdered, and if you want, you will be able to tell the captain for certain."

"How am I going to help you, Hamal? You're the sage, not I."

Hamal led him over to the body. Justice balked like a horse that didn't want to go near a snake, but Hamal tugged him forward until they were both squatting beside the casket, which, in addition to the body, was filled with shiny purple satin. It looked to Hamal like Ledaran's family had invested a good deal of money into his burial.

"Your name is Justice," Hamal said.

Justice looked at him. His face was still an odd color, and his voice was starting to sound tight, like he was speaking with hands wrapped around his throat. "I am aware of this. But what does it have to do with a dead patrolman?"

"Not every feeler can do what I think you'll be able to do." Hamal studied him a moment and saw how uncomfortable he was. "You don't have to do this, Justice, but I have known some feelers in the past who could put their hands on people and know things about them, the way a healer might. It depended on the name. I once knew a feeler named Trust, and he knew who could be trusted and who couldn't be trusted, just by putting his hands on the person. He worked for a prince, and his position was very important."

Hamal nodded toward Ledaran's body. "If this man died in a manner that was unjust, I think you'll be able to tell us."

Justice blew out a short burst of air that sounded like half a sigh and half a grunt of disbelief, but he proved he was brave. Without further hesitation, he reached out and set his large hand on top of Ledaran's chest.

No one among the watchers moved. Hamal could feel their gazes, Cale's especially.

"How will I know one way or the other?" Justice asked.

"Give it a moment," Hamal replied. "It always takes a moment, and I don't know why. There was one time, with Trust, when he had his hand on a prisoner for three minutes before he felt down in his stomach that the man was—"

Justice jerked his hand off Ledaran's chest and lurched backward. Hadley's guards quickly removed themselves from his way as he emptied the contents of his stomach all over the grave of someone named Marekar. When he was quite finished, he patted the gravestone as if in apology and then just groaned, not lifting his head.

"Well," Hamal said, looking up at Cale. "That's very interesting, isn't it? Trust said he could feel it in his stomach. He never told me he could feel it—well, *like that*. That seems to be quite a strong reaction, which is interesting by itself. Some feelers are stronger than others, you know."

Justice groaned again.

"But what does it mean?" Cale asked.

"It means," Hamal replied, "that when I put my hand on Ledaran's body, I will likely find that the captain was right. Ledaran was murdered. And he is due justice."

7 When Justice Came To Dinner

"How does one give justice to a man who is dead?" Cale asked.

They were riding home in the coach, with Justice on one bench and Hamal and Cale on the other, just like before. Justice was staring out the window, and he didn't look up when Cale broke the silence for the first time since they'd left Grower's Park.

Hamal waited for Justice to answer—his name was Justice, after all—but the feeler didn't seem to hear the question. So Hamal replied, "When justice comes, things are made right. That is what justice is like. Justice doesn't die when a person dies. Instead, it waits to see if someone will rise up to fix the situation and make things right again. We can't save Ledaran, but we can give him justice by making the situation right with his family. If you cannot make things right with the person, you can make them right with his descendants. That is how justice works."

"By arresting his killer."

"Well, yes," Hamal agreed. "That is one thing, but it would be better if we did many things."

"Many things?"

"If we're trying to bring *justice* to the bad thing that happened to Ledaran, we should do more than just find the man who did this. We actually need to make things right."

Cale blinked. "What do you suggest?"

Hamal looked over at Justice on the other seat. After a moment Cale followed his gaze. Justice didn't notice at first, and when he did, his head jerked around and he looked both of them with a distracted frown.

"Pardon?" he said.

"What should be done for Ledaran's family to make things right?" Hamal asked.

The frown deepened into a scowl. "Find his killer," he answered hotly.

Hamal had not forgotten Justice was a feeler, of course—but if he had, it was likely those words and how they were said would have reminded him. Justice carried fire within him as surely as any flamemaker. "Yes, of course. But after that? What should be done for the family *after* the killer has been arrested?"

Justice stared at Hamal for a long moment. "Was he married?"

"Yes."

"Children?"

Hamal remembered what Ledaran's blood had told him. "He had a son."

Justice nodded slowly. "How old was Ledaran?"

"Thirty-one."

Justice looked out the window again. When he gave his answer, his voice was quiet, as if he felt only a fraction of what Hamal suspected he actually did feel. "His widow should receive thirty years of his salary, plus a third more to compensate for her unexpected loss. The son should be allowed to take his father's position in city patrol when he is of age. If he wants it. Any of his other family members in need of assistance should be granted that assistance immediately."

"You are quite generous," Cale said, watching the feeler as only a seer could. Hamal didn't know for certain, but it seemed to him that his friend's words were some kind of test. Why was Cale concerned with whether or not Justice was generous?

"My answer is just," the feeler replied. "It is not justice unless it multiplies what was lost."

"I sense you're going to be expensive for the king," Cale remarked, his gaze still focused and studying.

It is a test, Hamal thought.

Justice chuckled deep in his throat. "No," he replied without any hint of anger or annoyance. The distraction slid away and he sounded quite sure of himself as he said, "I am going to do for the king the same as we do for Ledaran—I am going to multiply his holdings and turn South Barrow into the most prosperous district in his city. He will never again think of South Barrow except in wonder, and he will never need to lift a finger for anything he puts within my keeping. That is what I'm going to be for the king."

As if the words had physically reached out and poked him along the spine, Cale straightened on the bench. He stared at Justice, and Hamal almost asked what was wrong, what had surprised him so much. But he bit back the words and instead watched with wide eyes.

"That is a bold statement," Cale murmured at last.

The corner of Justice's mouth quirked in a partial smile. He turned back to the window. "You will find it to be true, my lord."

They returned to Cale's house, arriving at nine in the evening exactly. As they walked up the front steps, Hamal could hear the chimes from the large clock in the entry, and he noted that the clock had more to say than anyone else just now.

While still at Grower's Park, Hadley had made arrangements for Krasak to be brought to patrol headquarters and kept there. It wasn't an official arrest—not yet, but Hadley had questions only Krasak and a justice could answer. For the moment, Hadley had returned with them to Cale's house for dinner and to further review the case. Hamal didn't think Hadley had the opportunity to work with seers very often, so he immediately adjusted his plans whenever the opportunity became available.

They were nearly at the door when the captain said, "What I don't understand is how you knew Justice Hewen was in the king's prison to begin with."

Hamal took a breath. "Oh, yes! That's a very good question. How *did* you know, Cale? You didn't even have to think about it. When I said we needed a feeler named Justice, you knew exactly where to find one."

A servant opened the door for them, and they stepped into the entry. Hamal could smell wonderful things coming out of the dining room far off down the main hallway, and his stomach sighed in happiness, but it sounded more like a common rumble.

"Every few weeks," Cale replied, "I try to review the court files submitted to the king. From time to time, I come across a mistake made by one of the lower courts—a magistrate who didn't have all the facts in order when he made his judgment. As I read the report, I can see that its conclusion is false, though I cannot always see why. In that case, I arrange to have the prisoner brought before a justice, a man or woman with the gift, so the truth can be discovered. Two days ago, I read the reader's report on Justice Hewen, and though I did not find its conclusion false, I knew there was more involved in his case than what the reader reported. Specifically, I had the sense Justice was not a man we wished to keep in prison."

"What does that mean?" Hamal asked. "What were you going

to do?"

"Free him. Most likely tomorrow."

Hadley coughed once. "I see."

"It is kind of you to seek justice for those who cannot seek it themselves," Justice said to Cale.

Hamal smiled at those words. He knew that many people didn't *see* Cale when they met him; they saw only an important man who worked for the king. Justice was a prisoner with an incomplete sentence, but Cale still seemed embarrassed at the praise Justice gave him. He looked down the hall and started frowning.

"It is the least I can do. It's part of my duty to the king, as much as anything else."

Then Cale walked off toward the dining room, and Hamal had to hurry to catch up with him.

"Have you been doing this for a long time?" Hamal asked.

"Doing what?"

"Reading over the readers' reports from the Court of Justice?"

Cale shrugged one shoulder. "Since I started working for the king, yes."

"How many people have you saved?"

"Not many. Five or six over the span of several years."

Hamal stopped in the hallway. "Cale, that isn't a small number. That is a large number. You gave them back their lives. That is amazing. And it's important."

Cale flushed a strange color. "I know it's important, which is why I do it. But must we talk about this now, Hamal? We can talk about it later in private, if you wish."

"Are you embarrassed again? Why are you embarrassed?"

"Just go wash up for dinner, Hamal. You had your hands on a body today."

Hamal did as he was told and then joined everyone but

Justice in the dining room. In typical feeler fashion, Justice took quite a long time scrubbing his hands in the water closet.

Satha was waiting in the dining room, and she was wearing a lovely blue dress and pretty pearl earrings. Now that she could see, she chose clothing in an entirely different manner than she had before. All the browns and other earthy colors were gone, and she loved bright colors as much as she loved painting. It seemed to Hamal that she had just sat down at the table and he assumed she had, for she was a seer, and seers tended to know when other people would show up for dinner.

"I trust you had a successful venture," she was telling her husband.

"Indeed," he replied, sitting in the chair next to hers.

"And did you bring Justice Hewen back with you?"

"Yes. He is attempting to wash away today's encounter with a dead man."

Captain Hadley gave his greetings to Satha and bowed low, as you were supposed to do with a member of the king's family. He politely called her Lady Falreth, which always made Hamal a little sad. Her proper name was Lady Lehman, for she was Cale's wife, but for some reason Hamal could not fathom, this was unlawful in King's Barrow. She was from a noble family but Cale was not, and so they weren't supposed to marry. She only "visited" him here in the city and spent most of her time with her parents in Brannack or with friends up in Port Morden, on the coast.

Hadley sat down across from Cale and Satha at the long table. He was just telling Satha a few details of the case when Justice stepped into the room. The feeler came within four paces of the table before stopping still, his eyes wide.

His naturally low voice sounded rather high as he said, "Satha?"

All conversation about the case dropped into a puddle

of surprised silence on the floor. Cale stared at Justice with narrowed eyes, and Satha looked at him just as strangely. There was not a hint of recognition anywhere on her face. Hamal didn't think she knew him, but Justice certainly seemed to know her. He hadn't even bothered to call her Lady Falreth. Instead, he treated her the way Hamal would treat her, calling her by name.

"By the gods," Justice sputtered. "What happened to your eyes? You're a *seer*? When did this happen? I say, Satha, I'm...I'm quite surprised." His head tilted and he said again, "You're a seer?"

It was the sound of his voice, Hamal thought later. She didn't know his face—how could she have known him by his face? She used to be blind—but she knew the sound of his voice. Her chair scraped the floor as she slowly pushed it back and stood up with caution, her head cocked as if she were listening to something deeper than the words. Recognition struck in full and she jerked.

"Justice," she said. The word pulsed with shock, and her hand went to her chest as if she meant to keep her heart beating. "*You* are the feeler Cale had released from prison?"

Justice kept asking, "Why are you a seer? When did this happen?"

"About six weeks ago, when we met Hamal."

"Why are—? Oh. Hamal." Justice blinked and seemed to come to his senses. "I was in prison six weeks ago. No wonder I heard nothing about it. But a *seer*, Satha. How extraordinary." He started nodding but slowly, as if his thoughts still required sorting. "It makes sense, you know. You always did have keen intuition. I learned years ago that if you recommended someone to me, I should listen. And Hamal's a sage, but I must say, I am still surprised that you are—"

"Satha."

Satha and Justice looked over at Cale.

"Do you know Justice Hewen?" he asked, looking back and forth between them.

Satha's chin lifted slightly. "No, I do not know *Justice Hewen*," she replied, giving the feeler a reproving look. He shrugged both shoulders and smiled calmly. "But I do know a friend who is supposed to be studying law at the university in King's Bay. Cale, Hamal, Captain Hadley—may I introduce his lordship Justice Ashby, the son of Governor Ashby of Port Morden. He is a nobleman."

8 Justice Tells His Story

Justice was a quiet man. Hamal realized this all over again when he wanted the story, but Justice would give it only in pieces. He just wasn't a storyteller. It was as if he thought only certain points were important, and in his mind, there were only four or five of these important points; everything else was just details.

Over the evening meal, Justice told them he had been living in South Barrow for six months before his arrest. He had left the university and traveled down with a friend, a feeler named Steadfast. Hamal noticed he didn't call the man his servant, though that was what his file called him.

"I first heard about the conditions of South Barrow when I was a boy," Justice said. "Someone facetiously called it the *Poverty District*, and I thought they were serious. I remember being confused and thinking it should have a different name." There his flow of words ended, and he returned to his meal.

Everyone watched him as he ate—he had very nice table manners—and then Captain Hadley muttered something, and Cale sighed, and both seers started talking at once.

"You spoke to a relative," Satha began. "An older man with white hair and spectacles."

"Your uncle," Cale added. "We want the details, Justice. Please share the full story and tell us what actually happened."

Justice looked back and forth between Satha and Cale. "My uncle was the Minister of Finance for Cedrick's father. I learned from him the history of the barrow and what happened to sink the barrow into severe depression. After studying the issue and comparing my findings with those who completed their research before me, I realized there would be a relatively simple way to begin to improve the barrow's health. So that is what I set out to do." He shrugged. "Or it is what I was in the process of doing when I had a disagreement with a city patrolman about how he was using a building."

No one said anything until Satha leaned forward and used her stern voice. "Justice Ashby! You are less forthcoming in your stories than Hamal is."

Hamal jumped at the mention of his name. "Me? How am I a part of this?"

Her voice instantly softened. "You never tell everything you know, Hamal dear. And you, Justice, expect us to be content with a *shadow* of a story. You do not even give us the complete plot."

Justice smiled. "You're a *seer*," he retorted, calm and easy. "I thought all you required was a shadow."

"Were you always this irritating and I never realized it?"

"You used to be blind. I was being polite."

Hadley slung his napkin next to his empty plate and demanded, "So in your perspective, you had a *disagreement* with Krasak? How would you handle yourself if a sincere argument came about?"

But the heated words didn't seem to disturb Justice in the slightest. He put his head back and laughed, and everyone at the table looked at him in surprise. The laughter went on for a moment, but then it stopped, and Justice began to look at Hadley rather severely.

"Krasak," he stated, "would not vacate a building I purchased in South Barrow. It was my property. I didn't know who he was until I went to rectify the situation and discovered he was holding a dozen citizens against their will—men he was about to ship north to Druis Ephram's mine. Our 'disagreement' arose when he would not release them. He was destroying the lives of honest citizens on *my* property—he is fortunate all I gave him was a disagreement."

Justice turned to look at Cale. "That is the day I learned Druis Ephram's name. Krasak displayed such confidence in his scheme—and in his ability to continue his scheme—that he told me exactly what he was doing and why. And his confidence was proven correct. Steadfast and I were arrested for attacking a city patrolman, and that patrolman walked free. What happened was unjust and it remains unjust."

That simple statement was how he ended his speech, tinged with passion. He reached for the stemmed glass sitting near his plate, and it seemed he had nothing further to say.

Hadley took a deep breath. "What—?"

Cale held up his hand. Just as it was earlier that morning in the king's council meeting, Cale moved and all other conversations ceased. Hadley made way for him. It was interesting to Hamal how quickly people gave Cale whatever he wanted, or even what they thought he wanted.

"Hamal," Cale said, his silver gaze intent upon Justice. "You ask the questions. Whatever you deem important." And then, as if he could hear what Hamal was thinking, he added, "Anything."

Hamal looked over at Justice as a servant replenished his plate. Justice was a big man and it was good, Hamal thought, that he didn't pretend to eat like a small man. Pretending to be something he wasn't at a rich man's table wouldn't be good for him.

Justice looked at Hamal, waiting.

"What happened to Steadfast?" Hamal asked.

A moment passed before Justice replied, "Krasak shipped him north with the others."

"How do you know? Is it because he didn't come to see you in prison?"

"No. It is because *Krasak* came to see me in prison."

"Excuse me?" Hadley sputtered. He calmed quickly, but his face flushed scarlet and he gave Cale a look Hamal didn't recognize.

"Yes," Justice replied. "He told me he had completed his shipment and included one more—my friend Steadfast. Apparently, he spoke to the magistrate and had Steadfast released into his custody. A work release of some sort, he called it. But he told me exactly what that meant and what a feeler would endure in the Ephram mine."

He said these things without emotion, as if he gave a simple report that did not affect him, but his eyes told a different story. Hamal could see the heat building there and knew Justice was barely restraining his feeler's heart in this matter. He was right to be concerned. A feeler trapped in a mine filled with men who had been sent there unlawfully? It would not be an easy place for him. He would feel what they were feeling; it would be like a knife to the heart, which was something Hamal could describe in detail. He knew exactly what that felt like.

"But Druis Ephram was arrested and the mine was shut down," Hamal said, trying to encourage him. "Steadfast will be returned to you in a short time."

Justice nodded but said nothing.

Taking a deep breath, Hamal asked next, "Why do you call yourself Justice Hewen if your name is Justice Ashby?"

"Hewen is my father's name. My mother married into the House of Ashby. Both names are correct, but one carries the weight of the governor's seat and one does not. I should not be spared a prison sentence simply because I had the good fortune of having a beautiful mother who married well. Though my mother does not come from a noble house, the governor found a way to bend the king's law, and he married her anyway."

After a quick glance at Cale and Satha, Hamal nodded to show he understood Justice's reasoning. "You said you know what to do with South Barrow. What are you going to do with it?"

Justice's tension eased. Hamal watched the fire sputter out in the feeler's eyes, replaced with an excited light that was almost boyish. "I read a book by your grandfather. It was called *The Fall of Kingdoms*, and he wrote about the actions of kings and how they determine the fortunes of their people. Have you read this book, Hamal?"

Hamal laughed. "My grandfather has written more books than I have ever seen. I've heard of this one, I think, but I have not read it. What does he say?"

Justice broke a piece of bread in half and leaned forward to swipe it through the oil dish, being careful not to drip on the table. He had nicer table manners than Hamal did. Hamal found it very hard not to drip things on other things.

"The book is all about justice," the feeler said, leaning back in his chair. The bread disappeared. All of it, all at once. "I learned more about the true workings of justice through that book, one single book, than I ever did at the university. I was studying law—Shel Galen's book was coursework for us. One book out of many. But I read it and realized what the problem with South Barrow was. It was a lack of justice. There is no justice in South Barrow."

Hamal looked again at Cale, who was watching Justice and frowning thoughtfully. They knew those words. Cale was the one who had said them first—weeks ago. *There is no justice in South Barrow.*

"What do you mean?" Rewording the question, Hamal asked, "Why do *you* say justice is needed in South Barrow?"

"Shel Galen wrote that justice is a prophetic force. That is, it exists outside of time." Justice pointed a large finger across the table at Hamal. "I heard what you said in the coach this evening, Hamal. You summarized one of your grandfather's main points quite nicely. The need for justice doesn't die when a person dies. It waits for someone to fix what is broken. I don't know where you learned that truth, but I learned it in your grandfather's book."

He was teasing him, wasn't he? The look in his eyes, the humor. Hamal nearly laughed—what was it about Justice that made him want to laugh? It didn't matter that Justice had just been speaking of harsh things, of sad things; Hamal still wanted to laugh. "So what about the injustice in South Barrow?"

Justice nodded. "There was not one act of injustice but six. It began a year before the Barrow Wars, when the owner of a South Barrow factory was murdered by another factory owner."

"The Raldan case," Cale said.

Hamal noticed the words were spoken almost like they'd been stored up in Cale's head, waiting for a chance to escape. He couldn't tell if Cale knew the information because of his gift or if he had known it for a long time.

"What's the Raldan case?" Hamal asked.

"Raldan was murdered by another lord," Cale explained. "Another factory owner. The king responded by placing an interdiction upon both companies, closing them and putting thousands of South Barrow residents out of work." Cale scowled. "Tensions were already high between South Barrow and North Barrow. South Barrow was the factory district and was, in fact, the second wealthiest district in the city at the time. But the jewelers of South Barrow felt that the jewelers of North Barrow were placing too many restrictions upon them. Then when the king forcibly closed both companies, they were outraged. A year later, the Barrow Wars tore the city apart, and most of South Barrow set themselves against the king."

Justice nodded but held up his hand, first finger lifted. "*Most* of them. Not all. Five companies—five lords—refused to support the war against the king. They honored him, even though he acted foolishly. However, after the war ended, the king punished South Barrow by stripping them of their rights. Every factory in the district ended up being closed, including the few that had supported the king in the war. He acted unjustly against those who had supported him. Conditions have been deteriorating in South Barrow ever since. Now the barrow is truly destitute."

"The Barrow Wars ended two hundred years ago," Satha said, eyeing Justice intently. It was the searching gaze of a seer, who could see much more than other gifts expected. "How do you intend to right a series of wrongs that occurred two hundred years ago? Many others have attempted to aid South Barrow and, in the long term, have been unsuccessful. What will you do differently?"

Justice's lips parted in a grin. "Others have done great and noble works. They've poured a substantial amount of money into the barrow and tried to provide education and training for its residents. Those things are important, yes. But according to Shel Galen, what the barrow needs—what it requires—is justice. I am going to return what was stolen."

"You speak of the building Krasak commandeered," Cale said. He studied Justice much as his wife did, his gaze probing and alert.

Justice smiled again. "I bought it from the city, along with five other buildings in similar condition."

"You bought the factories."

Justice's eyes twinkled. "As I said, I have a plan."

9 What They Found in South Barrow

The light of the half-moon spilled across South Barrow like a whisper. Hamal had walked the streets of this district dozens of times, but in his memory, they always seemed a little brighter and he could see things more clearly. Tonight they wore more shadows than light and the air felt skittish, like a horse that was about to run away.

A sorry night for feelers, he thought. If Hamal could feel the tension in the air, what would Justice feel if he were here? It was a good idea to leave him at the house in North Barrow, if for no other reason than this—the way the air felt. It could be like this sometimes. South Barrow was not a healthy place for feelers to live. But putting a feeler in charge of South Barrow? That was different. That would make the heaviness leave.

After slipping across the bridge into South Barrow proper, Hamal and Cale traveled five or six long, empty streets until they reached their destination. The hour was just after midnight, Hamal thought, but he didn't feel tired. It was hard to feel tired when he was on an adventure.

He and Cale stepped beneath the shadowy overhang of an abandoned little shop and waited. By and by Hamal began to twitch, but the wait ended up being a short one. A shadow peeled away from the old warehouse on the other side of the street and walked toward them, disappearing and reappearing in the jagged cuts of moonlight. A fire long ago had destroyed some of the buildings here, and the moon shone through the charred bones.

"Evening, Commander," came a familiar voice.

"Good to see you, Will. What did you find?"

Oh, Hamal thought, delighted. *It's Will Chiodo.* Cale hadn't sent just anyone to find out about Krasak; he'd sent his charter. Charters could find anything, as long as it was touching the ground, and their gift made them wise. Most of them liked living in the country—in the North Woods in particular—but Will Chiodo was an exception. He had been working for Cale for five years. He and Hamal had talked about it because it was quite rare to find a charter outside the North Woods. It was even more rare to find one who was willing to live and work in a city.

"Odd things," Will replied, keeping his voice low. "You told me to look for a city patrolman who is a jeweler. That was simple to do, for there is only one jeweler in South Barrow who wears a patrolman's boots, and he received some unpleasant news today. A flamemaker ran a long distance to meet him, and after the man gave his report, your man Krasak turned and kicked a nearby wall—which accounts for the strange scuffmarks on the toe of his right boot. He's a kicker. That's for certain."

"Any idea of the news?" Cale asked.

"No, but I can tell you two things. The runner came from somewhere in North Barrow, and Krasak has abandoned his post. He boarded a ship for Riverstone around ten o'clock tonight and left the city. Whatever news he received today, it was enough to drive him away and it drove him fast."

Hamal could barely make out Will's face in the shadows. He tried to reason through this information on his own, before Cale had to explain it to him. Krasak was a city patrolman who did bad things. What sort of information would scare a man who did bad things? What had happened today that was important? Something had happened in King's Barrow, in the North Barrow district, and it had been enough to frighten Krasak away.

Hamal gasped. *Justice.* That was what had happened today— Justice had been released from prison. Was it really that simple?

When Cale said nothing, Will continued, "I cannot track a man on water. I am as blind as any other where water is concerned, so I let Krasak go. I can tell you the name of the ship and roughly how many men sail on her, if that's helpful. But here is the part I found interesting, Commander. Half an hour before he sailed, Krasak sent a message to the House of Ephram."

The House of Ephram? Hamal stared at Will in the darkness. "He sent a message to Druis Ephram? Doesn't he know he's not at home?" For his many crimes against the king's subjects, Druis Ephram lived in a cell in the same wing of the prison where they had found Justice today. It was not the good side.

When Cale finally answered, he pronounced his words slowly and in a distracted manner. "That case is over. Ephram was arrested, and those he stole are in the process of returning to the city." He paused and his voice grew quiet, like a whisper. "Why... would Krasak still be involved with the House of Ephram? There is no case. It is over."

"He's afraid," Hamal said.

Instantly he felt Cale's seer gaze pushing against him.

"Who?" Cale asked.

"Krasak. He's afraid of Justice. Justice was released from prison today." Cale didn't give his thoughts on the matter, so Hamal said, "Don't you think so? When Justice was in prison, Krasak stayed. Even after Druis Ephram was arrested, Krasak stayed. But he ran away today—the day Justice got out of prison.

He isn't afraid of the House of Ephram. I think he's afraid of Justice."

For a moment, Cale just looked at him, and Hamal began to wonder what he'd said that was so remarkable.

Then the seer breathed, "By the gods." And whirled to Will. "Today, when Krasak heard the news—where was he? Take us there."

They ran through the streets of South Barrow, unmindful of thieves or troublemakers who could be waiting in dark places. Will brought them to a street Hamal didn't recognize after his long run; the large building standing at the end of it didn't look familiar to him at all.

Will pointed at the building draped in shadow and moonlight. "That is the old light factory. Several of the back storage rooms are filled with supplies that haven't been touched in years. Exactly what the crates hold I cannot tell you, but I can say that as of this afternoon, the building was occupied. In fact, it has seen a good deal of activity for a supposedly empty factory."

"And right now?" Cale asked. "What is the count as of this moment?"

Will dropped down into a squat and set his hand on the street. A moment passed in silence while he listened to the earth, and then he looked up and replied, "Four."

Cale sputtered at those words. "Only *four*? How many occupied the building when Krasak was still here?"

"Sixteen."

Hamal's heart jumped. Cale sounded so alarmed.

"Describe the current occupants," Cale instructed.

After another brief conversation with the earth, Will replied, "They are a jeweler, a healer, a fairly large flamemaker, and—" He paused. When he spoke next, his voice had tightened. "And a justice."

Cale let his breath out in a rush. "A justice."

Will ran a hand over his mouth and muttered, "In South Barrow? Why would there be a justice in South Barrow?"

"Best way into the building?" Cale asked.

"Front door. There. To the right." Will motioned toward a long, narrow overhang whose shadows revealed nothing. "You will find all four individuals grouped together in the main room. Follow the first hallway and you'll see the doors. But, Commander, if I may? Perhaps it would be better if you waited for the next patrol." Will pointed at the factory again. "That flamemaker is not a patrolman, but he is some kind of guard or soldier. And he is large. The next patrol will pass by in five minutes—faster, if I go fetch them for you. I am not certain if it is safe to enter here without armed support."

But Cale waved the offer away. "There is no need for the patrol. I have Hamal."

With that, he walked off toward the building, and Hamal had to run to catch up with him.

"What is the matter?" Hamal whispered as they walked up the moonlit street. "Why are you nervous?"

Cale groaned. It was a sound like nothing Hamal had ever heard him make, and the seer replied, "I fear Krasak is vile— more so than Justice knows. I don't see how we will be able to make this right."

Hamal sucked in a breath. "What has happened?"

"We need to get inside and take a closer look."

When they reached the main door, Cale tried the handle and discovered it was unlocked. Easing the door open slowly, he slipped inside and Hamal followed him into a receiving room of some kind. Moonlight fell in through the windows, revealing a large room that was mostly empty, its contents raided and carted off long ago. The only things that remained now were a broken desk and a lopsided chair that had been shoved against one wall.

The hallway opened up just beyond the desk. Cale hesitated in the entrance, standing there for a moment as he peered ahead into the formless shadows. Hamal watched him, waiting. Eventually the seer seemed to make up his mind about something, for his back straightened and he strode forward as if he had with him an entire patrol, like Will had mentioned, and not just Hamal. Hamal followed along behind him, wondering about objects and broken things he couldn't see in the dark, and gradually they came upon a thin line of golden light trickling underneath a set of double doors. He began to hear voices. A man's voice in particular.

"…need to draw up a new set of plans. We could do *much* more in here than I was expecting. We could do exactly what he wants with this building—exactly. We could make it the finest point in King's Barrow."

Another man said, "We are still waiting for the signatures from the court. Do not forget this. The occupant may be gone for the moment, but that doesn't mean he won't return."

"He won't return," said the first man.

A pause. "And what makes you think this?"

"My unshakeable optimism."

Oh, Hamal thought. *That must be the jeweler Will was talking about.* When jewelers became focused on something, they fully expected it to happen. *Optimism.* That made sense. What did this jeweler want with Justice's building?

There was a healer somewhere in there, too. Hamal began to sense him as they drew closer to the doors. It was like being able to feel the sun on his skin. Whenever he felt it, he knew what it was. He could always recognize another healer. The awareness slowly became so distinct, so noticeable, that he could have told

Cale exactly where the man was standing on the other side of the doors. And his name—Hamal could have told Cale the man's name, too. Hamal always knew their names. He knew the name the way he knew the person was a healer. But other healers didn't always seem to know his name, and he didn't know why. This one was called Michal.

When they reached the pale light sliding out beneath the doors, Cale stopped. He turned to face Hamal and whispered, "Ready?"

Hamal wasn't certain what "ready" meant in this instance, but he nodded and braced himself.

Cale set his hands to the doors and shoved both of them open at once.

Light split the night. Someone had gone to a good deal of trouble lighting the main room. There were lamps everywhere, glowing brightly.

The voices cut off as the doors swung wide.

Hamal and Cale stepped inside.

The healer named Michal appeared to be somewhere around seventy years old. He had shoulder-length gray hair that he tied back with a cord. As Hamal and Cale walked in, he whirled around and reached for something at his belt. A weapon, perhaps. But he did not draw it.

The flamemaker, however, the large man Will had warned them about—he definitely drew a weapon. Hamal didn't even see him do it. His hands lifted and there were knives. It happened that quickly.

The jeweler was forty, perhaps a little older, and his broad shoulders suggested he enjoyed manual labor. He was a man who worked hard, Hamal thought, and did things with his hands. Beside him stood a woman. Will had not mentioned a woman, but he had mentioned a justice, someone with the gift, and

Hamal assumed this was she.

Cale walked ten paces into the room and stopped.

For a moment, no one said a word.

The jeweler's face twisted in a snarl. "So he has *seers* working for him now?"

Cale did not seem alarmed by the jeweler's response. He studied the man, his eyes narrowed as he used his gift. "I understand you're looking for Justice Hewen."

The woman reached out and set her hand on the jeweler's arm. It seemed to be a calming gesture, and Hamal noticed the jeweler responded well to it. Some of the fire blinked out in his eyes, but his expression remained full of disgust. He seemed to think he knew exactly who Cale was and why he was there.

The woman stepped forward, looking at Cale with the same kind of focus he used with the jeweler. If you had nothing to hide, the justice gift liked you. That was the way the gift functioned. And Cale was not a man who hid from justices. Hamal wasn't nervous for him, even though this woman looked fierce.

"Yes," she said simply. "Do you know his whereabouts?"

"Yes," Cale answered in the same tone she had used. "I do."

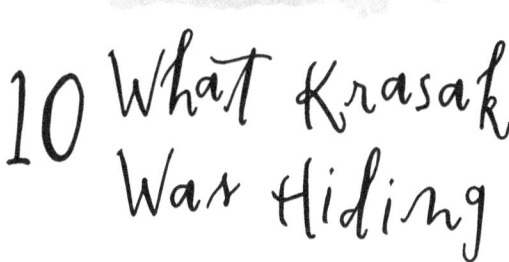

10 What Krasak Was Hiding

"Hello, Chestirad," Cale said, his voice calm.

Hamal had no idea who Cale was talking to. Then the big flamemaker guard sighed and began returning his knives to their various places on his person. He looked disappointed that there wasn't going to be a fight after all. It was obvious the man had been in plenty of fights before. His nose had been broken multiple times, but it seemed he had left it to heal on its own. It took Hamal several seconds to realize the man wasn't scowling on purpose. This was just his natural look.

"Hello, Commander," the flamemaker answered, and his companions looked at him in surprise. "Forgive the odd manner of our welcome, but you were not the man we were expecting."

Cale nodded. "I know the one you were expecting," he said and his silver gaze swept over the jeweler again. "But you can remove Krasak from your thoughts and plans. He has left the city."

"Ah," Chestirad replied, again ignoring the others and how they gaped. "Well, then. This is beneficial information."

"He was keeping you from accessing this building?"

"Yes. He filed paperwork with the city declaring that the

building had been purchased unlawfully. And with Justice Hewen missing, we could not contest him." Chestirad turned toward the jeweler. "This is Cale Lehman, former captain of the prince's guard and a man devoted to the king. I met him through Captain Hadley, of city patrol. Commander, this is Corin Groff."

Hamal straightened up. Corin Groff? He knew that name. Justice had written a letter to Corin Groff this very day, and now here he was standing in Justice's building. Did Groff know Justice had written him? It was possible he didn't, because the letter had been sent to a house in another district.

"You're his architect," Cale said, watching Groff.

Groff nodded.

The justice stepped forward, lifting her hand to gain Cale's attention. "You said you know where...?"

She stopped speaking as Cale bent down and rapped his knuckles three times on the wooden floor. Everyone stared at him strangely, but he acted like he didn't notice. He stood back up and said, "Please continue."

"Do you know where Justice Hewen is? You've seen him?"

"I have seen him. He is currently staying at my house. I've also heard his plans for South Barrow, and I can tell you with certainty that any paperwork that is delaying your project will be completed tomorrow. In the morning. All of it. I will tell you everything I can. However..."

He turned his attention back to Corin Groff, who was frowning like he didn't fully believe what Cale was saying. Hamal couldn't blame him because just a few hours ago, Groff had been fighting Krasak. It was hard to switch from a fighting frame of mind to a friendly one.

"Was the building empty when you arrived tonight?" Cale asked the jeweler.

It took Groff a moment to reply, "Yes. Why do you ask—ah,

my lord?"

Cale pointed across the large room to a door visible on the distant side. "Have you examined that room yet, Mr. Groff?"

Groff followed his look. "No, not yet." He cleared his throat, and his voice dropped a few notes, growing deeper and a little rougher. It was the voice of a jeweler who knew what he was about, Hamal thought. This was his natural voice when he wasn't so startled. "The original plans call it the second storage room. There isn't anything back there. No exit. Not even a window."

Cale's hand lowered. He was frowning at the door.

Hamal heard footsteps behind him and turned to see Will Chiodo coming hurriedly into the main room, blinking against the light of all the lamps.

"Yes, Commander?" the charter asked.

Chestirad's scarred, mean face brightened into something that almost resembled pleasure. "Hello, Will."

Will looked over at him, blinked again, and said, "Oh. Chestirad. I see you finally found a healer to fix your limp. I didn't realize that was you."

The big flamemaker grinned like Will had given him a compliment. It was difficult to confuse a charter. Hamal knew this was true.

Groff looked back and forth among them. "I cannot help you, my lord, if you do not tell me what is happening."

"Something vile," Cale murmured, and Hamal remembered what he had said before—about Krasak, about what Krasak had been doing.

The seer set off across the floor, weaving his way through the many lamps spread through the room, gathered up in patches as if someone had tried to make an odd kind of garden with them. Hamal ran to catch up with him.

They were within twenty paces of the door when Hamal

noticed for the first time that it hung slightly open. Every other door in this place was closed tight but not this one. A few more steps, and the stench hit him like a sudden wind in the face. Cale paused, lifting his hand instinctively to hover near his mouth. Hamal heard startled gasps behind him, and he thought, *Oh, no.*

He knew that smell. But many years had passed, thankfully, since he had stumbled into it like this.

As the others hung back, Hamal stepped up to the door and pushed it open the rest of the way. The action vaguely reminded him of opening up one of the tombs in Grower's Park, except this tomb had not been cared for. Instead, the room had been filled with horrible things and then closed up, left alone without thought or concern. Hamal's heart throbbed at the familiarity, and his eyes stung at both the smell and the shock. This was not good. This was not something that should ever be found in King's Barrow. Not anymore.

Light fell through the open door and exposed a large storage room that was completely empty. There were no bodies, no ropes or chains, but the room was rank with pain and terror and hopelessness. Hamal could feel all these things in the air. The floor was stained in horrific patterns that clearly revealed each place where pain had been realized.

Still and morbid, the air felt strangely heavy. It was the feel and stench of a slave yard. Of people whose souls had been stolen from them. *Something vile,* Cale had said.

"What *is* that?" Groff growled, sounding highly offended.

The words had a curious effect upon Hamal's heart. He wanted to pat the man on the shoulder and tell him he knew why Justice had chosen him as his architect. If Corin Groff didn't recognize this smell, if he didn't instantly know what it was, then he'd had nothing to do with it in the past. He might be a gruff, scowling jeweler, but he was an innocent jeweler, too. Someone

Justice would like.

"People were trapped here," Hamal explained when Cale did not. "They were held against their will. It always smells the same."

"What does that mean?"

"It means Krasak was turning people into slaves, and they didn't want to be slaves," Hamal replied, and after that, Groff stopped asking questions.

"Will," Cale called.

The charter stepped forward. "Commander."

"I cannot see that anyone died here."

Will seemed to hear a question Hamal did not, for he answered, "As far as I can tell, only one person has ever been killed in this building, but the death was not recent. It occurred several decades ago during a scuffle between a weathermaker and a flamemaker in the front room."

Will said these things as if he had the history of the building memorized. He was standing up straight, with his boots on wooden floorboards; he wasn't touching the earth at all, not directly, and Hamal wondered how much information the charter carried around in his head at all times. He was like a reader who had read a book about the city, but that book was written from the perspective of the soil under everyone's feet.

"Whoever was held in this room," Will continued, "likely walked out of it alive. Or if they died, they did not lose their blood. The earth cannot tell me of a death that did not happen on soil or, if it happened indoors, that did not leave blood behind."

He stepped up next to Hamal and looked over Hamal's head into the storage area. "Blood was spilled in this room but only in small amounts. It isn't enough to suggest a death."

When Cale spoke again, his voice was eerily quiet. "How many people has this room held in the last six weeks—since Druis Ephram's arrest?"

Hearing the strange notes in his voice, Hamal glanced at him.

Will also looked at Cale. He stayed there, holding his gaze for a long moment, and answered, "I cannot tell you with certainty, Commander. But I can tell you that when the messenger reached Krasak this evening, Krasak left in a wild fury and this room emptied. Krasak's companions deserted the building, and the occupants of this room left hurriedly on their own. I saw two of them in person on Bains Street. Two men—a weathermaker and an archer. They left the factory and went the length of three streets before finally parting company at the Ghost Bridge. Every person who was in this room today has returned to his or her home."

"Could you tell me where these homes are located?"

Another pause on Will's part. "Yes. But I would need some time."

Cale nodded, saying nothing more. Hamal could not imagine what was churning in the seer's thoughts.

Hamal could see Corin Groff starting to shift his weight behind Cale like a bull about to charge one of its herders. The man was upset and rightly so; he didn't understand what was going on in the building he was supposed to be working in.

Neither did Hamal. Not fully.

"But, Cale," Hamal said, "Druis Ephram was arrested and the mine was shut down—so why was Krasak still taking people? There is no mine for them. Is he sending them to a different mine? A different place?"

"If you wanted to buy a slave, where would you go?" Cale asked. His voice still hung low in the air, like a creeping thing.

Hamal tried to think through the question. *A slave.* If he wanted a slave. He didn't want a slave, but *if* he did—few places on the continent still embraced slavery. Theraine had never been a nation of slaves, not even in their infancy. Instead, they made use of bond servants, which was a similar concept in some ways, but the people could do whatever they wanted when their time of work was finished. They could leave their former masters and go somewhere else, or they could choose to stay with them. Many bond servants grew to be quite wealthy in Theraine because their masters came to know them well and trusted them to oversee their businesses. King's Barrow had made slavery unlawful just ten years ago, and some parts of the nation were struggling to survive without it. Cale had explained this to Hamal.

"Dasken," Hamal said at last. "If I wanted to buy a slave, I would go to one of the provinces in Dasken that still allow slavery. They have a history of slaves in Dasken, more than King's Barrow."

Cale's voice lowered even more. "And if you wished to *sell* a slave? Where would you go then?

The justice gasped. Hamal heard the strangled sound and turned to look at her, seeing shock that quickly turned to anguish. Hers was a noble gift, one that ruled well. Even an angry justice or a frightened justice would still care for the people around her. That was the nature of her gift. *There is no such thing as a bad justice,* Hamal remembered. Their gift made them concerned with the lives of others. They were like growers in this way.

Will was the one who finally explained. He sighed the air from his lungs and rubbed his dirt-covered hand wearily across his forehead. "So Krasak never stopped. When Druis Ephram was arrested, Krasak simply chose another market."

"Krasak is selling slaves in Dasken?" Hamal asked.

Cale turned to the justice. The motion was so abrupt that she jerked her head back and stared up at him with wide eyes.

"Thirty-two," Cale said, looking at her. "The total number of men, women, and children this room has held in the last six weeks is thirty-two."

She blinked at him. And then slowly shook her head. "Thirty-four."

That, it seemed, was the correct number. She nodded this time.

Oh, Hamal thought, remembering how it could be. *Seers and justices.* Cale could suggest what was true, and the woman could confirm it. A justice knew what was real and what was not real, so if a seer wanted to make certain he understood what he was seeing, he could ask a justice, who would be able to tell him whether or not it was true. Cale hadn't missed by much. He was doing well on his own. Hamal felt proud of him, even here.

Will sounded tense as he asked, "How will we be able to correct this situation? Even with a seer, how is it possible to recover those who have been sold as slaves in a foreign country? What can be done?"

The factory grew so quiet that Hamal, even though he wasn't listening for them on purpose, began to hear the heartbeats of those around him. Cale's was steady, powerful; he was upset and rightly so. The justice's heart—Hamal still didn't know her name—sounded aggravated, as did the hearts of the healer and the jeweler, though their angst was a little different than hers. They sounded startled, angry. She sounded sad.

Cale took a breath and let it out in a sigh the entire group could hear. When at last he answered, his voice matched the pace of his heart. He sounded certain. "We will give the matter to Justice. These are his people now. We will see what he will do with them."

11 The Prophet of Theraine

Hamal and Cale walked into the king's study the next morning as the large clock in the hall chimed six. Cedrick was already at his desk. He had a black mug of steaming tea in his left hand and a quill in his right as he signed the papers his secretary set before him.

The king looked exhausted, and Hamal wondered if he'd slept as little as they had last night, which wasn't very much at all. Because he was a healer and he thought like a healer, it occurred to Hamal that he could heal the king and make him feel more alert. Surely being a king would be easier if you felt good while you were doing it. But the king had his own group of healers—talented men and women who looked after him faithfully, so Hamal hadn't ever put his hands on Cedrick. Not even once. He thought sometimes that Cale wished this were different—that he wanted Hamal to examine the king, even if it was brief—but so far no one had asked Hamal to do so.

Norris Orissar, the king's secretary, was a lanky man with gray-rimmed spectacles and thick white hair that leapt off his head like the fur of a wild beast. Hamal paid special attention to him because he remembered how Justice had written him a letter just yesterday. It was quite possible that letter was sitting now upon the king's desk, somewhere within the carefully arranged stacks of papers. The king's desk was always tidy.

Lord Meles Colbis, captain of the king's bodyguard, was also present, looking strong and formidable next to the door. He nodded to Cale and Hamal as they entered. Hamal nearly inquired after the captain's daughter, a weathermaker named Quint, but the captain looked like he was mildly annoyed about something, and Hamal decided it wasn't the kind of face that wanted anyone to ask questions. At least not right now.

Once the door was shut and the five of them were alone, the king set down his quill and leaned back in his chair. He settled his mug in his lap, gripping it loosely with both hands, and looked at Cale with a shrewd gaze. "You were right."

Cale paused. Hamal saw his body freeze up like a bucket of water left on the northern coast in winter. Slowly the seer sat down in the chair on the left, directly in front of the king's desk, and looked at the king with narrowed eyes. "It came?"

What came? Hamal wondered, sliding into the other chair.

"It came," the king confirmed and expelled his breath in a long sigh. "This morning, by ship and courier. A single page, just like you said, marked with the Theranian royal seal."

Cale's gaze dropped to the papers neatly positioned on the king's desk. He waited, his face still, but then his hand twitched— his right hand, the one Hamal hadn't been fully able to heal. As if he couldn't help himself, Cale asked, "What did it say?"

The king didn't answer the question. Instead, he gruffly asked, "What do you know about Justice Ashby, the governor's son?"

Cale blinked the way he did when he was trying to sort the different pictures he was seeing. "He is part of the reason we've come to see you at this hour." His heart jumped and Hamal heard it. Cale's voice lifted a few notes, and it didn't really sound like him as he asked, "Did he…did he write about Justice Ashby?"

The king reached over and lifted a piece of parchment from the top of the closest pile. It was covered front and back with tiny, cramped words, written quickly by a hand that surely must have been tired afterward. So many words, squeezed onto a single sheet of parchment.

Hamal saw the parchment for only a moment as it moved in the king's hand, but that was enough. He took a startled breath as he recognized the handwriting. A firm hand, one that liked writing in tiny spaces. He knew who had written this letter.

No wonder Cale was excited.

"He did," the king replied. "In a manner of speaking. First, he *highly suggests* I listen to whatever my seer has to say about Justice Ashby. And then he mentions him again briefly at the end." The king looked at Cale across the desk, both brows raised. "This letter is unlike anything you've read in your life. He is as sporadic as a windstorm on the North Sea. In the middle of telling me what he thinks of the growers of Theraine, he pauses to write about goats. Apparently, keeping goats is good for the soul, especially if you're a grower. Then he talks about cakes that are made with goat's milk instead of cow's milk, which mightily impresses him. And if I ever have a chance to taste a cake made with goat's milk, I should definitely take the opportunity. He seems to write whatever comes into his mind, and it doesn't come into his mind in any form or fashion."

Hamal grinned. Yes. That sounded correct. He scooted to the edge of his chair. "Cale."

Cale looked over at him. So did the king.

"The Prophet of Theraine. That's who you're talking about, isn't it?" When Cale nodded, Hamal exclaimed, "You knew he was going to write the king a letter? And then he did? That's amazing! You really are the best seer in King's Barrow."

Cale grinned and he laughed a bit, but his gaze immediately went back to the prophet's letter in the king's hand. He was using his gift, watching the parchment as if it were alive.

"This is a highly convoluted letter," the king continued. "As this is my first direct contact with a prophet, I will tell you I am surprised. I've heard what it can be like to deal with a prophet, but I did not realize I would be able to see it so clearly in a single letter. At the end of his missive, the prophet finally ambles his way to his point. The reason he is writing in the first place."

The king gestured to them both. "He *says* he has information regarding your case with Justice Ashby. What that information is, he doesn't say, but it is clearly important to him and he refers to it as his *case*. The last thing he writes is that his case and your case will show themselves to be the same case in the end. Though exactly what that means, I couldn't tell you. He would like you and Hamal to go to Riverstone as soon as possible, so you can help him with his *case*." The king sighed again.

Riverstone? By the prophet's request? That would be exciting.

As Hamal looked back and forth between the king and the king's seer, the room began to feel...thick to him, as if something stirred just on the other side of what he could see with his eyes. Something was happening and he couldn't tell what it was.

Cedrick frowned at Cale for a moment and then dropped the letter onto the top of his desk. "And you are to leave on the same Theranian ship that carried the courier." The king started shaking his head. "The prophet was polite, as you may imagine, but it is quite clear that he fully expects me to turn my seer and my sage over to him without hesitation. The Prophet of Theraine has spoken, and may the gods protect us all if I refuse."

Yes, Hamal decided all over again. *The king is quite tired today.*

"The Prophet of Theraine requested us personally?" Cale

asked. He sounded rather interested and Hamal tried not to smile. Of course the seer would be interested in what the prophet was doing. One was like a puppy and one was like a pony, and they both liked to keep an eye on the other. If you put them together in the same room, they would always notice each other first.

The seer gift was rare. Cale said there were only eight seers alive in the whole of King's Barrow right now, but compared to the prophet gift, eight seers was a full clan. The prophet gift was one of the rarest gifts in the world. The Prophet of Theraine carried that title because he was the only prophet in Theraine. He was, in fact, the only prophet on the continent just now. They were such a rare gift that when a prophet took the time to tell you something, it was a good idea for you to listen. A prophet could direct kings if he wanted to, if the kings were wise enough to listen to him. And Cedrick was wise.

"Yes. By name. Both of you." The king sipped his tea and frowned. "Are you willing to travel all the way to Riverstone to follow a prophet's word?"

Hamal didn't realize he laughed out loud until all four men—Cale, the king, the white-haired secretary, and Captain Colbis—turned to look at him. "Oh," he said, straightening up uncomfortably. "I am sorry. I didn't mean to…you know."

"Why do you find that question amusing?" the king demanded.

Hamal felt a mighty flush take over his face and throat. "Well," he said, trying to be as polite as possible. It was good to be polite with kings. "Prophets and seers are always interested in one another. I think Cale is quite excited that the prophet has asked for us, and that's funny to me. Just look at him—he's excited."

The king's brows came down low over his eyes. He did not look at Cale. "It is my understanding that the Prophet of Theraine is difficult to see, even when he's asked for you. Working with a prophet is vastly different than working with any other gift, Hamal. Prophets are unpredictable, and right now you are in the middle of a council. You have business here in King's Barrow. Are *you* comfortable with abandoning your position to accept the untimely, unprecedented request of a prophet that may or may not come to fruition? If you go, you may not even get to see him."

Hamal looked at the king. Blinking in confusion, he shot a quick glance at Cale and then turned back to the king. "What do you mean, your majesty?"

The king's brows lowered even more. He didn't reply.

"What do you not understand, Hamal?" Cale asked.

"How are we abandoning the council?"

When the king just stared at him and didn't say anything, Hamal tried to explain his reasoning. "It seems to me that we did what we set out to do—we found Justice. You heard his plan, Cale, and you like it, so it seems like putting Justice on the council is a good idea. He can meet with them, and then you and I can go to Riverstone like the prophet wants us to. It's the same case! The council won't need us if they have Justice. And Satha will be here. He can ask her questions—you know, if he has seer ones."

The king was frowning again. "What do you mean you *found* Justice?"

Those words were like seeing a big orange cat in the middle of the throne room. They didn't make any sense at all, and Hamal found himself truly lost. "Well…I mean we found him, like we said we were going to."

"Why did Justice Ashby need to be found?"

Did he not know? Hadn't Justice told him in his letter? Hamal looked at him and stuttered a bit and said, "He was the prisoner."

"What prisoner?"

"The feeler named Justice, the one we went to go get out of prison yesterday—that was Justice Ashby. He was calling himself Justice Hewen, so no one knew he was the governor's son, but it was him. He was arrested for trying to stop a patrolman who was doing bad things. He sort of broke a few of his bones. The patrolman's bones, I mean."

A moment passed in which nothing happened. The room was quiet. The king and his secretary looked at Hamal, while Cale looked at the king.

The king stood up, his chair scraping the floor. "We had the *governor's son* in the king's prison?"

"Well, he's not there anymore," Hamal quickly replied and pointed at the closed door behind him. "He's out in the hallway with your cousin Satha. They're good friends. She used to visit his family up in Port Morden." He didn't mean to keep talking, but the words just came and he heard himself saying them. "We wanted to talk to you about Justice and what he wants to do in South Barrow. He has purchased some buildings and wants to give them back to the original families—he wants *you* to give them back, actually, because you're the king. Cale has many things to tell you, and we thought maybe you would want to meet him. To meet Justice."

The king blinked down at Hamal. His face couldn't seem to make up its mind whether to frown or not frown. He turned to Cale and repeated in the exact tone he'd used before, "We had the governor's son in the king's prison?"

Cale released his breath in a sigh. "It's a long story, Sire."

He told the king all of it.

12 The King's One Condition

Justice did look kind of scary, Hamal supposed. He was big and he had tattoos, and one of his eyes was missing. Hamal knew Justice and he knew what he was like, so he wasn't afraid of him at all, but Captain Colbis didn't know him, and it was his job to project the king from things that might be scary.

It took Cale an hour to update the king on everything that happened yesterday. When the seer was finished, Justice was called into the king's study, and Captain Colbis watched him with an intense frown, his hand on the hilt of his sword. Hamal wanted to tell him he wouldn't need the sword, but then he saw the look on the captain's face and decided that telling him wouldn't change anything.

Cale directed Justice to sit in the chair in front of the desk, which he did, and the room fell quiet as the king studied the feeler. Cedrick was a grower, and as such, he tended to be a good judge of people and what their hearts were. That was part of his gift. Justice sat there calmly, as if he knew exactly what the king was doing and was willing to wait for him to make his assessment. He looked incredibly comfortable, here in the king's study.

But then he spoke. "I broke his nose, your majesty."

The king's frown deepened. "Excuse me?"

"The city patrolman I assaulted. I broke his nose. I hit him one time and he crumpled like a dirt clod. The healer in his company had him back on his feet less than a minute later, and he walked away on his own strength." Justice's brows lifted up his forehead. "No one was more surprised than I to learn a broken nose had somehow become multiple broken bones and serious bruising all over his body. I do not know what happened to Krasak—if anything happened to him—but it was not my doing. All I did was break his nose."

Next to Hamal, Cale sighed deeply. "You've had multiple opportunities to explain the situation, Justice. Why have you not done so?"

Justice looked at him. "First of all, no one asked for my version of the story. If anyone in the Court of Justice had asked, I would have answered every question. But instead, they assumed the charges brought against me were true—exactly as they were presented. Second, the charges *are* true, though not to the extent they were presented."

Turning back to the king, Justice said, "I assaulted a city patrolman. Whether I broke his nose or every bone in his body, I assaulted him. The penalty for assaulting a city patrolman is four years in prison; that is the law. I knew that before I put him on the ground. I am explaining myself, your majesty, so you have all the facts and do not doubt your cousin's safety in my presence."

Sitting on the couch against the wall, Satha made a noise that was halfway between a groan and a laugh. "Oh, Justice. I appreciate the efforts on my behalf, but sincerely—stop. You don't have to prove anything here. Some three months ago, I sat in this very room, and over a pot of tea, I told the king all about you. He knows who you are and was actually considering giving you a position—before you disappeared from the university and no one knew where to find you."

The king frowned at her. "I never told you about the position, Satha."

"You didn't have to, Cedrick."

Hamal grinned. She had been a seer for six weeks. It was still new.

"My point is," she continued, "that Justice Ashby is well known in this room, with or without a charge of assault. For what it's worth, Justice, I appreciate that *you* were the one to hit Krasak. If you hadn't done it, Cale certainly would have, and I do prefer to keep him out of harm's way. For personal reasons."

As Cale turned a curious shade of red, Hamal laughed and Satha smiled at him, obviously pleased.

"Why," the king asked slowly, his attention on Cale, "would the patrolman lie about his injuries?"

Cale cleared his throat. "He worked very hard to make sure Justice was unable to contact anyone from prison, and he ran when he heard Justice was released. For the moment, Sire, I believe he lied about his injuries to ensure that Justice would be treated as a danger to others. That is, indeed, what Justice endured at the hands of men who should have protected him. Krasak presented a supposedly strong case against him, and his story was believed."

"And?" the king pressed.

Cale blinked slowly, staring at the king. "And when I find him, I will ask him. You know that Krasak took a ship to Riverstone last night, and I can tell you with certainty that he has contacts in the city who will be able to help him out of King's Barrow and into Dasken. He plans to enter the province of Rak-Min. That is where he intends to go. If we do not wish to chase him into the middle of a civil war, we will need to move quickly."

"A war, Cale?" Hamal asked.

Cale nodded. "The prince of Rak-Min and his sons were assassinated, and two members of his council have proclaimed themselves his successor. Each is building an army to support him, and already there has been much bloodshed on both sides."

The king sighed deeply. "You want to go talk to the prophet, don't you?"

Humor turned the corner of Cale's mouth. "I'm afraid Hamal was right about me, Sire. Yes, I do wish to speak to the prophet, but either way, pursuing Krasak to Riverstone seems like a necessary endeavor. I have told you of his activities in South Barrow; to the best of our ability, these things will need to be made right. I can have my charter work on locating Krasak's associates here in the city, but we would have more answers—and more justice—if Krasak were here as well. He will be able to tell us the names of his contacts in Dasken and potentially even the names of his buyers." Cale paused. "He will also be able to tell us why he warned the House of Ephram before leaving the city."

The king watched Cale a moment. Cale returned his look.

The room grew quiet.

"You are thinking of Darren Ephram, the son," the king said at last. "You are wondering about his loyalty to the throne, to the peace and safety of my city."

Cale moved in a way that suggested a shrug but not exactly. "You know my thoughts concerning Darren Ephram, Sire."

Hamal could hear it in his voice—one simple sentence could communicate a great many things. He himself knew nothing of Darren Ephram, but Cale certainly seemed to know him well.

Leaning back in his chair, the king waved his hand and said, "Introduce Justice to the council today at the beginning of the first session. Then go to Riverstone and arrest a former city patrolman who is about to have much more broken than just his nose. You will take a reader with you. That is my condition for this venture; I will know everything the prophet says to you, word for word."

"Yes, Sire."

They obeyed the word of a prophet.

Just after eleven o'clock, Hamal and Cale boarded the *Deressa Dalso* at pier number seventeen. It was a lovely ship with three tall masts and the golden banners of Theraine spilling from its ropes. Theraine built some of the most beautiful ships in the world, and they all had such lovely names. In Theranian *Deressa Dalso* meant "she who dances inside the sea."

"When was the last time you were in Theraine?" Cale asked as they leaned against the rail and watched the city of King's Barrow slide past them.

"A couple of years ago," Hamal answered, observing a little girl playing with a doll on one of the private piers. He waved. The girl lifted her hand shyly. "But the time before then, my grandfather and I went up into the Thalbrake Mountains and stayed with a family who had twelve children and twelve dogs. There were a great many dogs."

"What were you doing there?"

"My grandfather was researching one of his books. He travels a lot, my grandfather. He goes to many different places, and he is always writing."

Cale didn't say anything else until they were approaching the outer wall of the city. As its shadow fell across them, he asked, "Have you ever met the Prophet of Theraine?"

"Aye," Hamal replied.

Cale turned from the railing and gave Hamal his full, silver-eyed attention. "You have?"

"Yes."

"What is he like?"

It occurred to Hamal just then that maybe Cale was nervous. There was a small line between his eyes, and Hamal couldn't remember seeing it there before. He thought about what he could say to make him feel better and decided upon the best words possible. "He is one of the happiest people you will ever meet."

Cale blinked. "Happy."

"Yes." Hamal nodded. "Many prophets look at the pain in people's lives, or the secret things they're doing wrong, and they become sad or angry, or they try to make them do other things instead. Many prophets are depressed or sad all the time, but the Prophet of Theraine is different. He says there is always hope, so he will always speak hope. He encourages the people around him, so they are happy, too." Hamal shrugged. "He's happy. He is happy all the time…though I suppose I understand why some people are afraid of him."

Cale stared at him. "Why?"

"Well, because he can see all those secret things, too." Hamal chuckled. "He's like a reader who has read all your books, and now the words are with him always. But I don't think you should worry about meeting him, Cale. He is scary, but he is kind."

13 An Exception with Sages

They took a reader with them, as the king commanded.

Cale said it was standard practice to take a reader whenever you were on business for the king outside the city. You did this so the reader could record your activities and make a full report to the throne. Meeting with a prophet was, so it seemed, something of deep interest to the throne, so Cale had requested and been granted the reader of his choice.

The man's name was Gregory Almes, and he was unlike any reader Hamal had ever met, with the notable exception of his grandfather. Gregory was a short man, nearly as short as Hamal, but he was surprisingly strong. Hamal knew this because he'd bumped into him on the ship's main deck, in the part called the *stern*, and Gregory's body had told him things about muscles and sinews and a strict exercise regimen. Most readers were unused to labor. They sat around all day with their books, but this wasn't true of Gregory. His cloak was full of pockets and his pockets were full of tools. He carried *everything*, and when Hamal asked, Gregory happily showed him what he had stashed away. There were knives in there, plus writing utensils, a small hand shovel, needles and thread to "make small repairs as necessary," and entire books that were empty. He called them notebooks, "for making notes in." Hamal's grandfather carried books like these. The king would receive Gregory's notes at the end of the journey. Hamal found Gregory fascinating, and during their two-day journey to Riverstone, Gregory asked him lots of questions and would scribble his answers as fast as he could in one of his notebooks.

The thriving city of Riverstone sat on the border of Theraine. Most of the buildings were white marble, and the city looked elegant, warm, and golden in the light of the setting sun. Cale, Hamal, and Gregory waited on deck as the Theranian sailors made final preparations to put into port.

"Congratulations," Hamal said. "I've been meaning to tell you."

Gregory looked at him. "Congratulations? How so?"

He sounded so unaware that Hamal flushed. Perhaps he shouldn't have said anything. It was hard to tell sometimes when you were supposed to say something and when you weren't, but he and Gregory had talked so much the last two days that he hadn't even considered how saying this might be strange. Hamal rubbed the end of his nose and, because Gregory and now Cale were looking at him, finished with, "About the baby. Your wife is pregnant—that is what I meant. Congratulations."

"Ah," Gregory said and turned the deepest shade of red Hamal had ever seen on a living person. "Thank you, yes." He looked back to the docks.

He didn't seem to want to talk about anything else, which was quite strange, because he was Gregory the reader, and readers were always curious about things. Hamal's grandfather, Shel Galen, was curious about everything. Sometimes he even upset the people around him because he asked so many questions, but just now, Gregory seemed curious only about the docks.

A coach was waiting for them when they exited the ship. It was covered with intricate carvings that looked Theranian, even though they were still on King's Barrow soil. Riverstone was a bridge between two countries, and it had adopted many Theranian things, like the white marble buildings and detailed carvings. Nothing was plain in Theraine—they liked pretty, elegant things, and even the King's Barrow side of Riverstone reflected these tastes.

"He's married to a feeler," Cale whispered to Hamal as they climbed into the coach. Gregory stayed outside to speak with the driver. "It happened rather quickly, and he remains somewhat shy about it."

It could be like that sometimes, when certain gifts married other gifts. Sometimes it was hard to try to mix the different clans. Hamal wondered what Justice's stepfather, the governor, was like and what his gift was and if he had found it easy to make a feeler and her son part of his house.

"What's her name?" Hamal whispered back. "Gregory's wife."

"Adventure," Cale replied with a slight smile.

Hamal grinned. "Oh, yes. Of course her name is Adventure." That was the perfect name for Gregory. People said about feelers that when you found the name that spoke to you, no other name would do.

"Hamal," Cale said, now quite serious.

Hamal looked up at him.

"You remember that Theraine is a country of...specific rules that we must follow as closely as possible. We are on a mission for the king and it involves their prophet; we need to obey their rules as much as we can, even if we don't understand them. If we fail to do this, it could cause a diplomatic issue between two thrones."

Hamal knew what Cale was talking about. Theraine had *many* rules. The most important one was that it was very rude for foreigners to touch them. They were polite to foreigners, so long as those foreigners kept their hands and arms and other parts to themselves. "Don't worry, Cale. I will be good."

Cale gave him a funny look. "I wasn't telling you to be *good*, Hamal. I was just telling you what the king would say, if he were here. Kings have to be concerned with diplomatic manners. Sages, I am sure, worry less than kings, but as we are on a mission for the king, we need to be as diplomatic as possible." He paused. "How did you know Gregory's wife is pregnant?"

"His blood told me. A man's blood always knows when he has conceived, even if the wife hasn't told him yet. The blood knows things like this."

The door opened and the reader climbed into the coach. "They are taking us to a guesthouse on the other side of the river. Ambassador Torrek H'elm awaits us, but the driver would not tell me anything about the prophet. I am wondering, my lord, if there has been a change in plans already."

As the coach began to move, Gregory added from his resources of knowledge, "The prophet's gift is not known for its ability to think rationally. It looks at the future, not at what is conducive and constructive in the present. We may not get to see him after all."

"Timing," Hamal said.

Both men looked at him.

Hamal shrugged. "The Prophet of Theraine isn't good with timing. He is very good at prophecy, and he is very good at telling people things they need to hear, but he isn't good with timing. He's like me with numbers." Hamal chuckled. "Numbers are strange to me, and I can make very simple mistakes with them."

Cale stared at him. "Has…the Prophet of Theraine given you a prophecy, Hamal?"

"Aye."

Now Gregory was staring at him, too.

Hamal nodded. "Of course he has. He's a prophet—he gives everyone prophecies. I heal people, you know; that is my gift, but he gives them prophecies because that is his gift. He sees small things and big things, and whatever he tells you is important, even if it seems small at the time."

"What did the Prophet of Theraine tell you?" Cale asked.

"Many things. Things I am going to do. Things I will see. Some of it I don't understand at all, but everything he says is true and it *will* come true eventually, even if it doesn't happen when he thinks it will." Hamal shrugged again. "Timing. He isn't good at it."

Cale watched him with narrowed eyes, using his gift, but he didn't say another word until after they had crossed the Thalbrake Bridge and entered the country of Theraine. Riverstone was a large city that sat inside two nations. King's River cut the city into two pieces.

They reached their destination an hour after crossing the bridge.

"I understand," Cale said as he climbed from the coach, "that the Prophet of Theraine is quite fond of you, Hamal. You didn't mention you knew him that morning in the king's study, when we were discussing the prophet's unexpected request for our presence."

"Oh," Hamal replied. "Do you think it would have helped?"

There was a short paved walk between the coach and the front door of what Gregory had called the guesthouse. The building was, like its distant neighbors, made of white marble and covered with the same flowing etchings as the coach. *A nation of artists,* Hamal thought.

The air down here in Riverstone felt like rain without rain. It was thick and wet and gathered on your skin to roll down in rivulets. You started to imagine you could wring buckets of it out of your clothes with only two fingers, and it smelled heavily of flowers and spices. The air in Theraine always smelled of spices and other mysterious things.

Cale rushed his words so he could say them all before they reached the Theranian guards standing alert at the door. "I think you do not realize what it means for the Prophet of Theraine to send a letter to a man who does not expect one. Especially if that man is the king of another nation. The last time a prophet in Theraine sent a letter to the king of King's Barrow, it caused a good deal of confusion because twenty years passed before the prophet's word came about; it was twenty years early. So two days ago, Cedrick didn't know how to respond to the prophet's letter—whether generously and in good will or with concern. I cannot blame him for being cautious. Not every prophet can be trusted, though I do not speak specifically of the Prophet of Theraine." Cale eyed the guards in a way that suggested he was too polite to say what he was truly thinking.

Hamal didn't know what to say. He didn't know the story Cale was talking about, but he did know that if a prophet was going to be wrong about something, it was the timing. "He likes him," he said, trying to set his friend at ease.

Cale looked down at him. "Who?"

"The Prophet of Theraine. He likes King Cedrick."

Cale didn't answer for a moment. "How do you know this?"

"He told me."

They reached the front door, which the guards opened for them, and they entered a wide, spacious entry that was filled with the color blue. The soft rugs on the floor, the paint on the walls, the pictures, the marble statues—everything was a slightly different shade of blue, and it reminded Hamal of a house you would find near sand and water. A house meant for people who loved the sea.

"What did the prophet say to you exactly?" Cale asked Hamal, but just then the house steward arrived to welcome them and Hamal didn't have a chance to answer.

"My lords, thank you for coming," the man said, bowing as if he greeted them in the king's court. "His excellency waits for you in the rear garden with the evening meal and an apology. Those are his words. Please follow me."

An apology, Hamal thought. *Maybe Gregory is right and the prophet isn't here after all.* He sighed. It would have been good to see him again.

The steward led them through the large house and out into the garden, which was filled with flowering trees, blue and purple grasses, and hundreds upon hundreds of roses. Theraine was particularly fond of roses, which meant that all Riverstone was, too. A long table covered with a fine white cloth and multiple silver dishes with lids on them sat beneath a leafy gumroot tree. Every chair was empty. Hamal looked around for Torrek H'elm, the ambassador, and saw him coming up one of the paths through the rose bushes. He was an older man with kind eyes and long gray hair he kept tied in a tail that hung down his back.

Torrek smiled when he saw Hamal. "Why, Hamal. This time I see you come with friends."

Hamal laughed, recalling their last meeting. "I do! I am not so lonely this time, am I?"

Hamal took a step forward but then remembered Cale's words in the coach. This was a mission for the king, and while in Theraine he needed to follow the king's rules. So he held back for the sake of protocol, because the king would want him to. But Torrek didn't seem to know what Cale knew. He didn't seem to care about protocol at all. He held out his arms and greeted him as he always greeted him. Hamal returned his embrace.

He thought he heard Gregory—or maybe it was Cale—make a strangled sound behind him, but he couldn't be certain.

"It is good to see you again, Hamal," Torrek said and patted his back. When he let him go, he kept his hand on Hamal's shoulder. "It has been—what? Fifteen years at least."

"I never know," Hamal replied cheerfully.

Torrek laughed with all his chest and belly. It was a wonderful laugh, full of life. "Yes, yes. Oh, the similarities. I should like to see you more often, just so I can enjoy the similarities on a more regular basis."

The ambassador looked back at Cale and Gregory, who were staring at them. Cale seemed shocked. Gregory's face was red again. Truly, he seemed to blush as much as Cale. Torrek squeezed Hamal's shoulder and then pulled his hand away.

To Cale he said, "You will find, my lord, that we make an exception where sages are concerned." But then Torrek grimaced. "Alas, that is why the prophet has decided to return to his house in Shalas. He offers his apologies for not being able to meet with you at this time, but he feels it is more important for you to meet with someone else. After he laid out his reasoning to me, I found I agreed with him. This person will be able to conduct the prophet's case better than the prophet could himself. Gentlemen, may I present to you someone who has been a friend of my country for many, many years."

Torrek swung his arm toward the path he had just exited, revealing another man walking toward them. As Hamal recognized the man, he laughed in delight.

It was his grandfather.

14 The Sage's Request

To Hamal, his grandfather's face was perfect. It was a reminder of excellent things, of wondrous places and past adventures. It was the promise of a good future, because Shel Galen knew how the earth was run. It was knowledge, too—much, much knowledge; a reader's storehouse—but it was also the wisdom to know how to use that knowledge. Whenever he saw his grandfather, Hamal felt happy, because he knew good things were coming.

Shel Galen grinned. "Hamal."

Before Hamal could say a word in return, thick arms wrapped around him and lifted his feet off the ground, and he started laughing and laughing, which was always what happened when his grandfather greeted him this way. By the time Hamal's feet returned to the earth, he was out of breath and Cale and Gregory were staring again. Ambassador Torrek must have told them who this was because Cale looked surprised and Gregory looked like he might faint.

Shel Galen was a small man, like Hamal, but he was thicker and more muscled; he was a man who had worked hard all his life and had studied many different things that usually involved movement. His hands were calloused and he carried a sword named *Shaliar Mo'iantha*, which meant "the wisdom that divides" in Theranian. It had been a gift from Theraine many years ago, long before Hamal was born. Sometimes Shel had a beard and sometimes he had long hair, but he didn't have either this time, and he kept grinning and telling Hamal how happy he was to see him.

With a warm smile, Torrek gave Shel the names of Hamal's friends, and once everyone was seated at the table and servants were ladling up cold soups and using shiny silver spoons with the roast duck, Shel turned and looked at Cale.

"We don't have much time, so I will get straight to the point. I need to borrow my grandson."

Cale blinked slowly. Then he did so again. "Your—" he began and stopped. "Borrow him."

"Yes. I need to borrow him. You may come if you wish, and I would like it if you did. I could use you." Shel looked across the table. "And you, too, Gregory—though you will enjoy it less, I think. We will need to leave tonight at midnight, so we reach the South River by noon tomorrow."

As one man, Cale and Gregory paused. Their eating utensils lowered to the top of the table, and they looked at Shel as if he had put on a funny hat or a tunic that was full of holes. It was almost comical, this identical look on their faces. Hamal had no idea what they were thinking until Cale observed at last, "You are not like your...like Hamal."

Shel chuckled. He seemed to understand the comment perfectly. "All of us are different. That is one of the first things you will learn. Healer, reader, grower—all different. Yet in some ways we are the same. As a reader, I could not be like Hamal perfectly, and as a healer, Hamal could not be like me perfectly, but other things are etched in stone, and those things could never be different about us."

With a nod, Shel returned to the topic at hand. "The man you seek, this jeweler called Krasak, left the city six hours before you arrived. He is headed into the province of Rak-Min, where he expects to find shelter with Darsek Mi-lak, who just named himself the new prince. You will be able to arrest Krasak in two days' time, but Hamal and I need to leave at midnight, and I would like you to go with us, Commander."

Shel Galen knew many things he had never been told. It was always this way. He called Cale *Commander*, for Cale had worked for the prince, but the prince had died; the title of *Commander* was given to those in the King's Barrow military who had suffered great loss. It was a title of honor. Cale blinked again and turned to look at Hamal.

"Do you wish me to come with you and your grandfather?"

Hamal grinned. "Yes! I will always want you to come with me, Cale."

Shel grinned ruefully and shook his head. "You have known him for only six weeks," he said to Hamal. "He needs time. Seers tend to be suspicious of new people. It takes time for them to relax."

"Oh, Cale isn't suspicious at all. He is kind and wise and gentle. And brave. I think he is the bravest person I know—other than you, of course. How is *your* seer doing?"

"Oh, he's doing well. I had to leave him in Ra-Faal for this venture, but I expect to be home again in a few months. My seer is suspicious." Shel started laughing as if that word were an endearment of some kind. "He is *quite* suspicious. Of everyone. Most people would not call him kind, but I think he is kind, in his own way. And he isn't very gentle either. No one who knows him would use that word, but he is brave and he is wise. And he is very blunt, which I appreciate. Is your seer blunt?"

Hamal thought about it and stirred his soup with a carved spoon. "No, I wouldn't say he's blunt. He thinks about things before he decides to say them, and then he tries to say them in a way that is kind."

"Waiting to speak is a sign of wisdom."

"I think so, too."

"I enjoy being friends with a seer."

"So do I!"

"You are friends with one, and I am friends with another, and it happens to be both at the same time. A curious turn of events. I'm sure the prophet would have something to say about it." Shel's nose wrinkled in a familiar smirk.

"He has something to say about everything."

Shel laughed. "That he does. You know…" He gestured with the spoon. "Lately, he keeps talking about the Prophet of King's Barrow."

"Oh, he's talking about our prophet again, is he?"

"Yes. He has filled six or seven volumes about this man, going on and on about who he is and what he's done and what he will do." Shel waved the spoon over the table. "Not all of it makes sense to me, not yet, but I expect your prophet to be an interesting fellow."

"We don't actually *have* a prophet in King's Barrow," Hamal told him.

Hamal noticed Gregory wasn't eating. The man was scribbling as fast as he could in one of his notebooks, his head down, his arm and hand moving like a machine in an alchemist's shop. Then Hamal noticed Cale wasn't eating either. He was just sitting there, looking first at Hamal and then at Shel across the table. His brows were pinned halfway up his forehead, and his eyes were wide, and he seemed quite startled by something, but Hamal couldn't think what it would be. He was just about to ask him when Shel kept talking.

"Well, no, you don't. In a certain light, I suppose you *don't* have a prophet in King's Barrow." Shel shrugged. "But the absence of the Prophet of King's Barrow doesn't stop the Prophet of Theraine from talking about him as if he's already said hello and introduced himself. You know how he is."

"Timing."

"Exactly! He's always been questionable when it comes to his sense of timing, and this remains true when he's talking about another prophet. It makes him so excited to find another one that he can't help himself, I suppose."

"Do you know when our prophet is coming?" Hamal asked as he ate his soup.

"No," Shel replied, "not exactly, but I do know that he will be twenty-three years old when you are eighteen, so it will be soon. You aren't eighteen now, are you?"

Hamal shook his head. "I am seventeen."

"When will you be eighteen?"

"I don't rightly know. Next year perhaps. Maybe sooner."

"Then it won't be very long. Oh, that reminds me—you will find this interesting. Out of all the things the prophet writes about this young man in King's Barrow, this is what he repeats most often: *The sea courts his favor.*" Shel shook his head. "I don't know why they'd do such a thing. They have their own prophets—why would they need yours? Anyway, I don't understand it, but I don't need to. Not yet. The story lies with the Prophet of Theraine, and he can work it out as he usually does. I say, Hamal—what do you think of this soup? It is very good, isn't it?"

At the head of the table, Ambassador Torrek turned to Cale. It seemed he didn't think Hamal could hear him, for he spoke quietly and his lips were bent in a little smile. "One grows accustomed to it eventually. As much as one can."

Cale gaped at the ambassador. "How often have you experienced this?" His voice was not quite as quiet as Torrek's.

Torrek shrugged one shoulder. "A few times. Imagine sharing a meal with these two *and* the prophet—that is an adventure that compels the mind to stammer. The hours slide by in a heartbeat, and the ears begin to burn as the mind is unable to fathom the topics of gods discussed simply and easily by sages." He smiled again and then seemed to remember what he was talking about. "Shel is correct, of course. Our prophet greatly enjoys speaking of yours. He calls him the Great Mystery and speaks as if he has already been born."

Hamal missed some of what the ambassador said next because Shel asked Gregory a question about pencils. Ordinary ones. Gregory stuttered and stammered and eventually passed Shel the pencil he was using so the other man could examine it.

"But, your excellency," Cale began and stopped. A moment passed before he tried again. "A prophet of King's Barrow? We have never had a prophet within our borders. Surely, such an important happening would be known long in advance. And..." His face turned pink along the edges, but he pressed through and spoke his thoughts anyway. "The prophet gift does not come by accident, as you know. There are specific things that must occur before it appears."

A baby, Hamal thought. *Cale and Satha have to have a baby.* The prophet gift wasn't like other gifts; it came only from two seer gifts that produced children together. *Cale and Satha. They are the first seers to be married in King's Barrow in hundreds of years. Maybe ever.*

If the prophet would be twenty-three years old when Hamal was eighteen, it must be that Cale and Satha would have a baby soon. The baby would need time to grow up to be a man.

Torrek nodded. "Of course. I do not understand it either, but if you heard the prophet speak, you would know the certainty of his words. He is convinced your great nation is graced with a man of like gifting. The Great Mystery, indeed. That man will be the Prophet of King's Barrow. And the Prophet of Theraine is already fond of him."

Maybe that's another reason the prophet wants to speak to Cale, Hamal thought. *Maybe it's more than just this case with Krasak. Maybe he wants to talk to him about his child.*

15 The Intelligence of Shel Galen

They had completed the meal and were just starting to discuss the prophet's great love for goats when Shel looked up and called, "Oh, there you are. Were the streets crowded?"

Hamal twisted around in his chair to see a boy approaching the table. He appeared to be Hamal's age, perhaps a little younger, and he was thin like a healer or one of the other gifts that didn't often need to lift heavy things. When he saw the boy's hands, Hamal started thinking he might be a musician. The boy somehow reminded him of the feelers he had seen in the king's palace who played their instruments during dinners and special events. Feelers made excellent musicians. It was like they knew what their audience needed to hear—those exact notes and those exact words.

The boy stopped a few paces from the table and bowed elegantly like he had grown up in a prince's court, and Hamal thought perhaps he had. Shel knew all manner of people in all manner of places. Some of them had never seen a king's palace, while others never left the palace except with a hundred soldiers guarding them. Shel was friends with all these people.

"Yes, sir," the boy replied. "The first attendees are arriving for the New Moon Festival, and the streets are filling." He spoke the king's tongue with the accent of Dasken, which tended to drop the final Gs and slur syllables in the middle of words.

"Were you able to get word to her?"

"Yes, sir."

"Excellent." Shel turned back to the table. "The way is set for us, gentlemen. We will leave at midnight and meet our guide in Dasken tomorrow at the South River." The corner of his mouth pulled into his cheek as he added, "You will appreciate her. She is…unique."

The boy bowed and left.

Hamal didn't think anything more about the boy until ten o'clock that evening when he found himself alone with Cale. They were looking over a map of Rak-Min, a province filled with brittle, sandy ground and a series of stubby hills that eventually became Morden's Passage to the east.

They were alone in the library when Cale turned to him and said, "That boy tonight at dinner."

Hamal glanced at him. "The one who looked like a musician? He had the hands of a musician."

Cale frowned and leaned back in his chair. He looked over at the library's door as he said, "I am confused by something, Hamal, and I wish that you would tell me more about it."

"I will do my best."

"The boy is a feeler. His name has something to do with the mind, though exactly what I could not tell you. Knowledge, perhaps. It is a name that would cause him to do well with a man such as your grandfather, a reader. I have no doubts that your grandfather cares for him a great deal." Cale paused. "But your grandfather also owns him. He purchased him from a slaver in another province six months ago. Your grandfather—a sage—

owns a slave. I don't know what to make of this."

"My grandfather does many things people don't understand at first. But then they do."

Cale grunted. "I am certain that's true—but a slave?"

"Shel lives in Dasken. They allow slavery there."

"I am aware of this." Cale shifted in the chair and lowered his voice. "But how could a sage own a slave? For years we have worked in King's Barrow to remove slavery from the mindset of the average man, both the one who was a slave and the one who owned him. Yet your grandfather bought this boy as if—" Cale's brows rose. "Well, as if he believes owning slaves is wise. How could it be wise? Surely you would never own a slave, Hamal." The face Cale made clearly displayed his opinion of this idea.

Hamal looked at his friend, unsure how he should answer. At last he ventured, "I have been a slave. That's how I met Richart, you know. But I have purchased a few slaves in my lifetime, too. Their faces are still dear to me. Every single one."

When Cale just watched him, not saying a word, Hamal continued, "The first time, I was just a little boy, maybe seven years old. She was a pretty girl a little bit older than I, and she was about to be sold to a bad man who would have treated her in bad ways—in ways no one should be treated. So my father gave me money for her, and I bought her. She was my friend. We played together and did everything together, and when she grew up, she wanted to marry a jeweler who lived down the road, and so she did, and they had eight children. All boys." Hamal smiled at the memory. "I helped deliver them. Her descendants still live in the province of Ar Ran."

Cale still stared at him. "But surely you did not keep her as a slave. You purchased her to save her from an unfortunately common fate in Dasken—I understand that—but then you set her free."

"I don't know," Hamal replied. "I can't remember."

"How could you not remember?"

"It didn't really matter."

Cale opened his mouth, closed it, opened it again. "How could it not matter?"

Hamal began to think they were trying to have a discussion about two different things. Maybe what Cale pictured when he thought of slavery was different than what Hamal thought of. It could be like that sometimes, when two people came from two different places and then they tried to have a conversation about something they both thought they knew.

"She was my friend," Hamal said finally.

"Yes, you said that."

"If you're asking if I ever gave her a certificate of release so she could file it with the city leaders, and then everyone would know she wasn't a slave anymore—I don't remember. She never asked for one. I think she forgot."

"She forgot."

"Aye. It didn't matter to me, and it didn't matter to her because in the end, it wouldn't have changed anything. It would not have added anything to the promise I made her."

Cale blinked. "The promise."

Hamal nodded. "She was free the entire time. If slavery were still lawful in King's Barrow, some people might call me your slave."

Cale started frowning.

Hamal ignored him. "I was a poor boy living in South Barrow, and you took me in—some people might call me something you wouldn't call me, but if you did call me that, I wouldn't mind. I would be proud to be your slave, because it wouldn't be any different than it is right now."

"How can you say that?"

"I can say that because I know what I mean to you. Whether others call you my master or my friend, it doesn't matter because I know what I know. I look out for you, and you look out for me. I enjoy being with you. I don't care what the rest of the world calls it." Hamal laughed. "I don't even care what you call it, because I know what it really is. This is friendship and it is real. It is something important. I would give everything I am to you, if you needed it. That is the promise I have made to you, and I know it is the promise you have made to me. You would do the same for me as I would do for you."

Cale blinked slowly. "You are a sage, and I am your attachment."

Hamal grinned. "See? You can call it anything you want. It doesn't change what it is."

Cale studied him with silver eyes. "So that day in South Barrow, when we first met and you made the decision to befriend me, this is what you meant? You made a *promise* to me."

"Yes. And I did so gladly."

Cale looked away. Such a long time passed that eventually Hamal went back to studying the map, and he nearly jumped when Cale started speaking again.

"So you think your grandfather has made a promise to this boy?"

"Yes—of some kind. There are different kinds of promises, you know, but they all work out the same in the end. Shel is friends with a seer just as I am friends with a seer, but his seer lives down in Ra-Faal, far away from here. So the promise between this musician boy and my grandfather is a different kind of promise than what I have with you. But as he purchased this boy, then yes, he made a promise to him. A special kind of promise meant for a special kind of purpose."

Hamal thought of something else and exclaimed, "We should

find out what his name is! He's a feeler—if we knew his name, it might tell us what the promise is."

"Intelligence," came a voice from the doorway.

Hamal and Cale looked up. The musician boy stood next to a bookcase filled with works of history. Most were in Theranian, but a few were in the king's tongue, written so long ago that the spelling was strange and some of the words were barely legible. Hamal and Cale had been looking at this shelf of books just a few minutes ago. Somehow the feeler had entered the room and picked up one of these books—an exceedingly large volume with a painting of a camel on the front—and neither of them had seen him do it. Even Cale had missed the boy's entrance. How long had he been standing there?

"My name is Intelligence," the boy said in his Dasken accent, "but many people call me Tell." He looked at them almost as if he expected a question, and when neither of them said anything, he continued, "Forgive the interruption, my lords, but Shel has requested a book. There is something he wishes to show the ambassador."

He bowed low and left, book in hand.

Hamal and Cale looked at one another.

"Tell," Hamal said. "It rhymes with my grandfather's name. *Shel* and *Tell*. They go together."

"Intelligence," Cale mused, staring after the boy. "No wonder he has found a home with a reader. What sort of promise do you suppose your grandfather has made to a feeler named Intelligence?"

Hamal shrugged. He could think of only one thing. "It is a promise that will last a long time. How could it not? You're right about a reader wanting to be friends with a feeler named Intelligence—that makes perfect sense to me. I imagine Gregory will like him, too." He chuckled. "I also imagine it is easy for Tell to remember facts and details, the way a reader would."

"Perhaps," Cale agreed. His gaze was fixed on the empty doorway, his eyes narrow as he used his gift.

"What is it?" Hamal prodded him.

"There is something curious about that boy, something beyond his name and the fact that Shel Galen, a sage, purchased him from a slaver." Cale sighed and returned his attention to Hamal. "But I cannot see what it is. I feel like I know him. I look at him and I can sense the familiarity, though I know I have never seen his face before today. He is unfamiliar and familiar at the same time. Does he seem—not *look,* but *seem*—familiar to you?"

Hamal shook his head. "No, I don't think so. I have never seen him before."

"Well," Cale replied and blinked, looking away from the door. "Perhaps we will learn the answer to this mystery, too, before the end of our journey."

16 The Price of Silver

Just before the large clock in the hallway chimed midnight, Ambassador Torrek pulled Hamal aside to speak to him privately in a small sitting room. An ornate fountain trickled in the corner between two windows. Water flowed down an orderly pillar of rocks into a shallow pool filled with stones. There were many such fountains in the guesthouse, for Theranians were fond of fountains.

"Hamal," Torrek said, setting his hand on Hamal's shoulder. "You understand I will not be going with you into Rak-Min."

Hamal nodded. The Dasken desert was no place for Theranians and their great love for leafy, growing things. In addition to artists, many people in Theraine were growers—men and women and children who knew how to make beautiful things grow from the soil. There were many weathermakers, too, but even these preferred to stay out of the desert.

"This means," Torrek continued, "that I need to give you your message from the prophet now, before you go. He said to tell you that one is enough. Two are better, but one is enough. Sometimes all it takes is a day, and there are times when silver is worth more than gold."

Hamal waited, but Torrek just looked at him expectantly.

"That's all?" Hamal asked. "That's all he said?"

Torrek adjusted his grip on Hamal's shoulder. "He said you would know what it was about."

Hamal couldn't help but laugh. "I never know what it is about! Not in the beginning. The prophet is a complete mystery to me. Sometimes he says a great many things about something that is for only one person. Just one. And then at other times, he says only a few things about something that is for an entire country—hundreds of thousands of people, yet he said only one or two things about it. I never know what he's doing when he does it. His gift is beyond me."

Hamal thought about the many, many times in the past when he had received similar messages from the prophet—messages that just seemed like words strung together on a rope without sense or reason—and he shook his head. "But in the end, I start to understand. In the end, the pieces come together for me, and I can see what he was talking about. It is astonishing how the stories turn out every time, and he gives so much hope. Every time he speaks, his words are full of life, especially when you don't know what's going on until later. Especially then. It is good to figure out what he means in advance, so you can wait and watch for the good things that are about to happen."

Torrek agreed. "I am honored to call him my friend."

Hamal grinned. "I know he says the same thing about you."

"Until next time, Hamal. I look forward to seeing you again. Perhaps this time, it will be sooner than either of us expects."

That night, beneath the cool, pale light of a full moon, they left Riverstone and rode south, following the Theranian border on the King's Barrow side. For several hours, the road was good and large farms lay on either side. In the moonlight Hamal could see signs of life everywhere he looked. They passed mile after mile of healthy farmland and fenced-in pastures and groves of fruit and nut trees. *Growers live here,* he thought.

But as the sun began to rise, the land changed. The fields fell away into discontented earth that didn't want to grow anything other than straggly black-leaf bushes and the occasional desert oak tree. As Hamal examined the land curiously, he thought about the stories his father had told him of when the earth was different here. Riverstone was a garden now, but many years ago, when his father was just a boy, it used to be a desert. It used to look just like this—miles of dry earth and sand. People would ride camels in Riverstone. Hamal could barely imagine such a thing, especially now, with his visit to the city so fresh in his head. There was nothing of the desert in Riverstone now.

Shel had arranged for a team of rough-looking weathermakers to accompany them into Dasken. No one traveled this road without guards of some kind, and these were trained men who had obviously run this route several times. The weathermakers made jokes even while the sky was still dark, and they didn't seem to mind the threat of thieves and marauders. They appeared to be quite brave, but Hamal slowly noticed that they never relaxed. They carried as many weapons as Chestirad, the big flamemaker who had been looking for Justice Ashby back in South Barrow. He would fit in with these men; they would be friends.

They reached the South River on schedule. The little village sitting next to the river was quiet in the day's building heat, and a barge waited to take them to the opposite shore.

But the guide Shel had hired wasn't there.

"Did you tell them the north side?" Shel asked his feeler servant. "You specifically said the north side."

"Yes, sir," Tell replied.

For several minutes, Shel sat in the saddle and looked around the dusty terrain as if he could summon their guide with his gaze. When no one appeared except a skinny little boy chasing a dog, Shel turned to Cale and demanded, "Seer—where are they? Why are they late?"

Cale blinked at him—Cale was blinking a lot on this venture, Hamal noticed—and turned to look out over the dry ground. He nudged his horse forward a few steps and sat there, watching the land on the other side of the river.

Hamal waited and tried not to twitch. Sweat gathered on his forehead until he could feel it walking down his skin, and he swiped at it with his sleeve. The air felt like the bread room in a rich man's kitchen. So many ovens, all going at once.

Lifting his arm, Cale pointed southwest. "A small escort has been sent for us. The bulk of their party stays behind with a member who has been injured."

"What kind of injury?"

A moment passed while Cale squinted off into the distance. "A bone fracture, though I cannot tell you which bone. Something below the waist. Right knee, possibly."

Shel grunted. "Can't tell me which bone," he muttered and rubbed his hand over his mouth. He seemed to be thinking; this was his thinking face, and Hamal watched with interest, for he never knew what would happen when his grandfather was thinking about something.

Eventually Shel lowered his hand. "How long until the escort arrives?"

"Half an hour. Perhaps less."

"Then we shall meet them on the other side."

They followed Shel to the barge, where they loaded on five at a time and were carried across the river. Muscled weathermakers with sleeveless tunics and uncovered heads steered the barge through the gray-green water with long poles. It seemed they had done this plenty of times before, for the barge moved smoothly and they didn't speak to each other at all. They were like part of the barge itself.

When his horse nickered and stomped a hoof, Hamal patted the creature's nose and calmed it, brushing away its anxiety with his touch. The horse lowered its head into his hands, and chuckling under his breath, Hamal began to coo to it. "You don't like boats, eh? It's going to be all right. You'll be on dry ground again soon. No one is going to need to swim today."

Cale slid into the space next to him, stepping around the horse's shoulder. Hamal looked up and, grimacing against the sunlight, adjusted position so he could look at his friend without the sun full in his face. "I say, Cale..."

"Yes, Hamal."

"Are seers good with riddles?"

Cale smiled slightly. "That depends. What is the riddle?"

Hamal leaned toward him. Cale leaned forward as well and tilted his head so he could hear better as Hamal whispered, "What is better when there are two of them, but it is all right if you have only one? The prophet gave Ambassador Torrek a message for me, and that is what he said. Two are better than one, but one is enough, and sometimes all it takes is a day. He said something about silver, too. Silver is better than gold sometimes. That's my riddle. I'm trying to figure out what it means. The prophet said I would know, but I don't."

Cale was quiet. He turned his gaze to Shel, who sat upon his horse on the opposite shore. Shel and Gregory had taken the first barge across the river, and though the journey was short, Gregory had scratched notes in his notebook the entire way. Every time Hamal looked at him, the man was writing. Even last night on the road, Gregory had gripped a pencil in his right hand and a small glass shaft—a weathermaker's lantern—in his left, while balancing a notebook on his thigh. As soon as there was enough sunlight to see by, the reader had wrapped up the shaft and returned it to one of his many pockets.

When Cale spoke next, Hamal gaped at him.

"He speaks of Justice Ashby."

"Justice? How do you know?"

Cale tapped his own left cheekbone. "His eye. Justice has only one. The prophet is describing him."

"Oh," Hamal said, thinking about the patch Justice wore and how the socket had healed on the other side. "Oh, well done, Cale. I never would have put that together. The prophet must have known I would ask you."

"Yes, well…" Cale smiled, but his gaze remained intense as he continued to use his gift. "It would seem that Justice has had contact with something that is important to his case; the prophet references something Justice has *seen*. I cannot tell you the nature of this thing, whether it is an object, a person, or a situation, but I can say it is different. That is, it does not follow the typical standards of society. Silver is worth more than gold in this case. It has a higher value. In other words, Justice wants something that others would perhaps overlook."

"We already knew that about him," Hamal answered.

Cale looked down at him, and a quiet laugh rolled up his throat. "Yes, I believe you are correct. Justice always sees what others have left behind."

Swishing a fly away from his horse's ear, Hamal asked, "Do you remember how the prophet said that his case and Justice's case were the same case?"

"Yes," Cale answered simply.

"We're in Dasken now and Krasak is here—somewhere. We will be able to catch him soon, so that is good. But how are the cases the same?"

Cale let his breath out in a sigh that made Hamal remember how they'd ridden horses all night long and wouldn't be able to sleep until tonight. "I have no idea."

But then the seer paused. Lifting his hand, he shielded his eyes and looked back toward the shore they had just left, toward Riverstone. "Perhaps the prophet gave you this riddle for a reason."

"The prophet always has reasons for things."

"I mean that perhaps it is a detail we need specifically for this case. A clue. If, while we are in Dasken, you find something that is silver, but it is *worth more than gold*, take note of it. Come and tell me, because it may be important. Both for Shel's case and for ours."

17 Thunder in The Desert

They left the river behind.

The air grew heavy with a hot, dry Dasken wind that blew across the flatland. As Hamal ran his sleeve across his brow, he was glad they didn't have any flamemakers with them. Flamemakers were made for heat—for fire and combustion and searing temperatures, but they were made to *sense* heat as well. They felt it when it was outside their bodies and could be quite sensitive to it. When they were surrounded by intense heat like this, there were times when it started playing with their heads. Deep in the desert-like South Territory of King's Barrow, the flamemakers stationed at South Post had to be careful, or they could come down with something called *sand sickness.* They would see shapes and bright colors and things that weren't really there. Sometimes they would even hear voices.

The desert was better suited for weathermakers, who felt just as comfortable in the heat as they did in the cold. They could live in the desert or up on the northern coast, where the bitter winter winds could turn your ears black in less than half an hour. Both places were filled with weathermakers who didn't bother with scarves, head coverings, or coats. Rain or snow, heat or ice, it was all like a pleasant spring in King's Barrow to them. Hamal wondered sometimes what it would be like to be a weathermaker who never felt chilled or uncomfortably warm. He thought he would like it.

They were about two miles from the South River when Gregory rode up beside him. For the first time in hours, the reader was not writing. His face was an odd color that didn't seem to go with the light or the heat, and he spoke to Hamal in a low voice. "May I ask a question?"

"Yes," Hamal replied, curious. Was Gregory upset? Was this an upset face?

"It involves your grandfather." Gregory said the words almost apologetically, as if he thought Hamal might change his mind now that he knew the topic.

Hamal chuckled. Gregory was an interesting fellow. Hamal sometimes wondered if he needed someone to touch him—a hand on the shoulder or a pat on the back. Some people needed to be touched more than others, and sometimes those people didn't know it. "Of course."

Gregory hesitated. Drawing his horse as close to Hamal's as possible, until their boots brushed together in the stirrups, he whispered, "Your grandfather just corrected my spelling. For a word I hadn't written yet. I was about to write it, but I had not written it."

Hamal waited to hear the question, but apparently, it was going to be one of those hidden questions, where the speaker thought he asked something when he really hadn't. Gregory looked at him with wide eyes, and it seemed he had spoken all the words he intended to say.

"My grandfather knows things," Hamal replied. What else could he say? Shel Galen was a library. No, that was too small. He was a thousand libraries, each one built and preserved by kings and princes. Large libraries. Many libraries. He had more things in his head than any person alive.

"Even things he has not read?" Gregory breathed.

Hamal shrugged and repeated, "He knows many things. You can ask him about it, if you would like. He likes it when people ask him questions." Gregory looked a bit nervous about this, so Hamal added, "You could ask him how he knew what you were about to write. He would enjoy an interesting question like that."

Gregory just looked at him, his face filling, emptying, and then filling again with different expressions. Eventually, he reined his horse behind Hamal's and drifted all the way to the back of the line to mix in with Shel's hired soldiers. Hamal had no idea what had disturbed the reader so much. If he had a question, he should ask it. He had asked Hamal dozens of questions aboard the Theranian ship on their way to Riverstone. What was so different now? Gregory and Shel had the same gift—they were readers—so why was it that one was uncomfortable around the other? It didn't make sense to Hamal at all.

A short time later, they rounded a bend in the road and met up with their escort.

Four riders approached from around a distant hill. They had a healer with them. Hamal could feel him—no, he could feel *her*—as the riders came close. He waited, and slowly he began to sense her name. It was a Dasken name, something short and simple: Ji. She was rider number two in the group, on the back of a sleek black horse that tossed its mane and snorted as the two groups of people stopped together on the road. Hamal could instantly tell this healer had much more experience with horses than he did. The horse was big, yet it obeyed her instantly when she directed it to calm.

"Shel Galen," the first rider greeted.

Hamal looked through the group. They were all women—

weathermakers, by the look of them, for their heads and arms were bare despite the sun. Only Ji wore a long piece of black cloth called a *bassan* that desert dwellers—anyone who was not a weathermaker—often used to keep the sunlight away from their skin. Though Hamal looked over the group with interest, the only weapons he saw were a long knife and a bow. This group was as different from Shel's hired soldiers as it could be. One was all men and heavily armed; the other was all women and secretly armed. He was certain there were more weapons among the second group than what he could see. There always were more weapons in Dasken. It was safer that way.

"Hello, Kila," Shel returned. "Only four of you today."

The rider named Kila swore roughly, and Hamal nearly dropped his reins. Behind him, one of the soldiers grunted in obvious appreciation.

"Lost a rider," Kila replied. "A new girl. She wandered off sometime last night in the middle of Darsek Mi-lak's territory, and Emia wants to find her before Mi-lak does."

"Too late for that," Shel said calmly.

Kila paused but only for a moment. Her eyes narrowed as she fixed him with a steady gaze. "Pardon?"

"Mi-lak's men are growing bolder. She was on watch, I suppose? Yes. They took her while she was on watch and broke her knee when she refused to cooperate with them." Shel nodded toward Cale, and Hamal remembered what his friend had said about one of the riders having a broken bone. "That is their preferred method of communication as of late. Break the knee, negotiate, heal her if she agrees to their terms. I would keep this one, Kila. She's brave. Emia could use her."

Kila's head turned and she looked over at Cale. "Bah," she said at last. "You and your seers. I should know better than to trust you, Shel."

She sounded quite serious about the whole matter, but Shel put his head back and laughed heartily like she had amused him on purpose. "This one isn't mine, but he functions admirably all the same. Come now; we need to see Emia. We will be able to claim your missing girl tomorrow evening—you know where she is. We will have the opportunity to fetch her back."

Kila started frowning. "We were hoping it wouldn't come to that."

Shel's smile faded. "It is destined to come to that, *chila*. It must come to that. He does not know what it means to lead. He is not a man the gods have ordained to lead. You know what this is like and you dread it, just as I do."

She watched Shel until Hamal began to wonder if she was going to argue and use some of those colorful words again. But she didn't. In the end, she sat back in the saddle and released her breath. "Very well, if that is what you wish."

"It is what will occur," Shel replied.

Hamal had no idea what they were talking about.

"Emia waits for us near Pas-sik," Kila said.

Shel nodded. "We should hurry."

They rode south for three hours. The flat desert of Dasken began to dip and swell in a series of small hills that gradually became tall, dusty ridges of sand and stone along the horizon. This was Morden's Passage, and it was filled with old, old stories about thieves and dragons. Many books had been written about Morden's Passage, but Hamal didn't know how many of them were true. Not every story told in Dasken was accurate when it came to dragons, but it was true that Dasken knew more about dragons than King's Barrow did. King's Barrow hadn't had a dragon in centuries.

As they rode, an interesting thought came to him. Maybe

he should ask Gregory Almes about the dragons and the many stories that were written about them. Gregory would probably know.

Near a hill with a gnarled scrub oak growing out of its side, Kila left the road and took them east. Just a few steps into the desert, the earth grew sandy and began to sink beneath the horses' hooves, so they had to go more slowly. Hamal was beginning to think about supper when his ears registered an unexpected sound.

Was that thunder?

He looked up at the sky in surprise because all the heat and all the sunlight didn't match what his ears told him was true. The sky was perfectly clear. Not a single cloud marred the pale blue face that seemed capable of melting a leather saddle just now. Why would he hear thunder on a clear day? *A clear day,* he thought, squinting up at the sky. *Thunder on a clear day.* That seemed familiar to him somehow.

The answer came to him just as Kila cursed. His stomach jumped with the sound of her voice.

"Shel!" she hissed. "That's Emia. We have trouble."

A weathermaker in trouble, Hamal thought, taking a breath. He remembered it now—those terrible nights in South Barrow when the flamemaker clan and the weathermaker clan had fought over a warehouse or a street where they wanted to work. Thunder was sound and sound could speak; weathermakers could communicate back and forth with their gift. He didn't know what they said, but he had never met a weathermaker who seemed confused by the message.

His grandfather turned to Cale. "Seer."

Cale immediately began speaking. That wasn't like him, and Hamal realized he must have seen something before Shel asked about it. "Darsek Mi-lak's men have attacked your guide. Emia.

They have orders to fill his army for the coming war, and your guide does not wish to be among this number. This is getting to be a common occurrence in Rak-Min—conscripting men and women into military service."

Kila had plenty to say about this.

Shel let her shout. It was almost as if he couldn't hear her and the descriptive words she was using. He sat there with an annoyed look on his face until at last he sighed deeply and said, "Hamal."

Hamal pretended he didn't hear Kila either. "Yes?"

Lifting his hand, Shel motioned toward the next rolling slope and the battle they could not see on the other side of it. Thunder rolled—more loudly this time—and Hamal's next intake of breath smelled of smoke. Something burned; they had a flamemaker over there somewhere. Either that, or a weathermaker had started a brushfire with lightning.

"This fight is inconvenient to me," Shel stated, his voice carrying across the sand. "Make it stop."

Kila's flow of curses ceased.

Hamal felt Cale's gaze on the side of his face. Several of the others were staring at him, too, with brows lifted and heads cocked as if they needed to interpret what was a very simple command. Nothing Shel said just now needed interpretation, but both groups of soldiers looked at Hamal with expressions that could only be called peculiar.

"All right," Hamal replied.

He twisted around in the saddle until he found Ji the healer. She looked at him from beneath the dark hood of the *bassan*, which draped over her entire body and even flowed over part of her horse. The only parts of her Hamal could see were her face and her hands holding the reins. He realized suddenly that this was the first time he had seen her eyes and—for just a moment—

he forgot why he was trying to find her. What had happened to make her so sad? He could see the sadness as clearly as he could see her face.

"I will need you," he told her. "Come with me."

She rode out with him.

18 A Question of Blood

Hamal could feel Cale's seer gaze pushing into his back as they rode away. He wanted to tell his friend not to worry. Why would Cale be worried? Yes, there was a battle. There were people fighting and killing each other just on the other side of the next hill, but this was a healer's job: to bring peace. Often that meant bringing peace to a person's body, one body at a time, but sometimes it meant bringing peace to many bodies at once, which wasn't any harder—you just had to avoid being shot with arrows or lightning. It was good to avoid being shot.

Several times—at least four, when he thought about it—Hamal had walked onto a stretch of land riddled with pain and the loss of blood, and he had done as his grandfather requested: He had stopped the fighting. It was an easy thing for a healer to bring peace in the midst of pain. There was no reason for Cale to be concerned for him.

As thunder rumbled ominously, Hamal thought of Will Chiodo the charter and wondered what it would be like for a charter to walk across a piece of land that was covered in blood. *A charter would have trouble on land like this*, he thought. The pain in the earth would bother him.

Hills rose up on all sides. A sudden gust of wind, shocking in its winter-like coldness, blew sand in Hamal's eyes, and he was rubbing his face as they rode around the hill and found themselves in the middle of a melee. He had learned that word from Cale. It meant a fight that was confusing, and this one was wild.

First, you had the weathermakers, who tended to be a bit windy when they were upset or frightened. Hamal was used to wind in the city, when you had to duck around blowing leaves and twigs and other small items careening through the air. But an alarmed weathermaker in the desert was an entirely different matter. Get enough of them together, and you ended up with what Hamal and Ji were about to ride into: a small sand storm.

Gusts of erratic winds billowed from multiple directions. Hamal quickly gave up trying to avoid the sprays of sand and just hoped they wouldn't run into a lightning bolt, or an electrical charge, or a shard of ice, which could do more damage than a little sand in the eyes or lungs. Weathermakers were dangerous in a fight. They always were. They could really slow a healer down.

Then you had the flamemakers, who could be a little strange because of the desert heat. One time many years ago, Hamal had seen a flamemaker light his entire body on fire and walk across the sand with a sword in his hand. But the sword melted before he reached his adversary, so he had to turn around and go back. Flamemakers were dangerous warriors, too. In the desert their unpredictability made them more dangerous than their gift itself.

But there was one gift Dasken was known for. Just as Theraine was known for its growers and artists, Dasken was known for a gift that used the desert like a canvas or a theater stage, turning it into something it was not. Hamal peered through the flying sand and wondered, *Where are the thieves?* There were always thieves in Dasken, and many of them greatly enjoyed fights like this one. This was entertainment for them. Many thievers did not think about life and death the way the other gifts did.

There. Movement above his head.

He looked up into the narrow, triangular face of a dragon hawk. It was a very good likeness, too—each wing was as wide as a coach was long, and the sunlight shone through the thin red flesh of the wings as if it were fabric. Hamal could tell this thiever was skilled. The creature looked real even as it moved.

Beside him Ji hissed a curse and flung her hand out to grab his arm. He could feel her fear through her mighty grip. This is what thievers did best in fights—produce fear in their opponents. Even if you knew it wasn't real, even if you knew it was just in your head, it was hard to argue with your eyes. Many people lost their lives to thievers in the desert because they thought something was there, and it wasn't.

Hamal had seen dragons before. He didn't need to see them again—real ones or imagined ones.

He held up his hand.

The dragon hawk vanished, gone in a breath.

The sand cloud jerked as if it were a giant tablecloth and someone had grabbed hold of it on the other side. The wind died away. The sand grew still. Ji pulled her hand off Hamal's arm as quiet dropped across the battlefield.

Hamal could see them now—men and women standing across the sand, weapons in hand. Many of them were dirty, covered in sweat and blood. He could sense other healers on the battlefield, and as their names came to him, he called them out. "Abdan, Dalia, Daylid, Gadi, Safae—save the dying."

He didn't look to see if they did as he said. They were healers; eventually they would want to heal. It didn't matter who they worked for or what they had been doing a few moments ago, whether they had been healing people or trying to harm them. They could heal now. That was what healers did.

Sliding out of the saddle, Hamal went to the closest person and began to work on him. Shel could take care of the politics and *why* these people were fighting each other; Hamal much preferred this part—getting his hands dirty as he took care of the hurting. This man, a weathermaker, had been stabbed in the chest, and he gasped for breath from a punctured lung. Hamal cleared away the blood that was trying to drown him and spoke quietly to soothe him.

As he worked, his grandfather's voice came to him across the sand.

"Don't look so surprised, Seer. The healing gift will always be able to bring peace. That is what healers do. Peace to the body, peace to the mind." Shel lifted his voice. "Bring your commander and I will speak to him."

For a long, bitter moment, no one on the field moved.

The first to step forward was a woman. She was dressed in tan and gray clothing as if she hoped to blend in with the desert terrain, and she held a sword that emitted a strange light—something gray or silver. *A weathermaker,* Hamal realized as he worked on his patient. He wondered if this was Emia, the guide Shel had hired.

The man who eventually stepped away from his associates and came forward also held a sword, as well as a bloody knife in his other hand. He was covered in splashes of scarlet, and Hamal's gaze went to the many bodies in the sand he left behind.

As Shel began addressing these two people, Ji dropped down beside Hamal and began to heal the next person. She had chosen to heal a man, Hamal noticed; she was working on one of the people who had been fighting against her team. She had stripped off her *bassan,* her protection from the sun, and Hamal saw something that gave him a moment's pause.

Her arms were bare, and they were covered with tattoos. Tattoos of birds. Just like Justice Ashby's.

She made quick work of the man she was healing. She had talent. Hamal could tell. They moved to the next two—a male weathermaker who had a horrific gash in his leg and a female weathermaker who was dead—and Hamal asked the obvious question.

"What do the tattoos mean, Ji?"

She grunted as she healed the leg wound. It was a sound that suggested she had more important things to think about than what her arms looked like. She replied, the words terse, "This is how many people I defeated in the Blood Race."

Hamal had heard of it. It was a difficult athletic competition held in several key provinces in Dasken. People sometimes died, and with a race named after blood, he could only imagine what it was like. You would probably need a healer afterward. Maybe even during.

He healed the dead woman.

Ji froze as the dead woman began to gasp for breath beneath Hamal's hands. She had died from a fire bolt to the chest. Nasty business. Now she was going to have a strange scar in the shape of an angry flower. He had some trouble with one of the muscles in her back until he realized it was deformed—she had been born this way. It probably caused her a good deal of pain, considering her occupation, and he was happy to fix it for her, so she would be able to bend and twist like the gods intended.

"I know someone with tattoos just like yours," Hamal said as he closed a gash on the woman's head, behind her left ear.

Ji grunted again, but the sound was different this time. She kept looking at the woman Hamal had healed. "Not *just* like mine, I think. I was the Crown Holder that year."

Hamal grinned at the pride in her voice. "Oh, I don't know," he teased her. "It is close."

Hamal and Ji went on to heal a thiever with an arrow in her stomach, a weathermaker who'd lost his hand, an archer who had been hit on the head so hard that her brain had dislodged from its place, and several others. It was not the largest battlefield Hamal had helped clean up, yet the fight had been violent. The aftermath made his stomach feel tense, almost as if he had a stomachache, or what he imagined a stomachache would feel like.

Cale appeared next to him. "Your grandfather is asking for you."

When he had finished healing the man he was working on, Hamal climbed to his feet and wiped his bloody hands on an old piece of cloth Ji tossed to him. He had blood even under his fingernails. Being a healer was dirty work.

Shel and the others stood on the road with the hill at their backs. Sitting on the ground, as some readers did when they had much to write, Gregory Almes was filling a notebook with his sloping handwriting. Intelligence the feeler stood near his master, watching the proceedings with a slightly pinched look around his eyes.

"There you are, Hamal," Shel said.

The woman—the guide Shel had hired—looked at Hamal with a hooded sort of interest. He thought it was interest, but perhaps it was suspicion instead. It was hard to tell with her. The man covered in other people's blood did not look interested at all. He frowned at Hamal, giving him a look that almost felt like needles on the skin. He was not, so it seemed, a pleasant sort of fellow, and all the blood on his clothes and throat made the sensation worse.

The man spat, "A sage? This is nothing but a boy. You expect me to take you before my master on the word of a boy alone?"

"If you wish," Shel replied smoothly, "I will have this boy stop the battle again."

Hamal didn't know what his grandfather was trying to say. Battle? What battle? There was no more battle for him to stop, but the man—a jeweler, Hamal thought, because he was not windy and his skin was red from the sun—clamped his jaw and didn't say another word.

"Hamal," Shel said, "I understand that you were the personal healer of the House of Rayme. Is this true?"

Hamal could feel Cale's gaze again. It pushed on the side of his face almost like fingers. "For a time, yes," Hamal replied.

"And when did this occur?"

Shel never asked questions like this unless there was something he wanted someone *else* to know. He didn't ask for himself—why would he do that? He already knew the answer, and he knew it better than Hamal did. He remembered everything. He had been there, too, all those years ago when the House of Rayme was young.

"I don't know," Hamal answered. "I was just a boy then. Maybe nine."

The jeweler grunted.

The guide lifted both brows and glanced at Cale.

Shel didn't seem to notice these reactions. He continued, "You are familiar with the blood of Rayme."

"Oh, yes. I am very familiar with it. Blood doesn't change— it is more faithful than most people think. I would know any member of the House of Rayme, even the child of a distant cousin. I would be able to recognize him by his blood. Any healer would be able to do this."

A corner of Shel's mouth tucked into his cheek. "But most healers are not familiar with the original."

As Shel smiled like this—it was a look that said he knew

things—Hamal remembered what the prophet had written to the king. *A case.* They were here because of a case. Even if Hamal, Cale, Gregory, and everyone else forgot all about it, Shel would not forget anything. It was not in his nature to forget.

"I brought you, a sage, into Dasken so you could verify a birthright," Shel explained to Hamal. "That is why you are here. With a touch, you will be able to give truth to those who have shown themselves willing to fight for it. Their questions you alone can answer. You've stopped one battle. Now it is time for you to stop the entire war."

19 The True Prince of Rak-Min

"Is the blindfold truly necessary?" Cale asked, his voice low. He sounded nervous and Hamal glanced at him.

Shel Galen put his head back and laughed, his voice as open and free as Cale's was quiet and reserved. One of these men was uncertain about all of this, but the other was certain about everything—about his life, his path, his decisions. Shel was never nervous, and there were times when other people didn't understand him. He had been called many things in his lifetime, both good and bad, but he didn't care about any of them.

"Yes," Shel answered simply. "I have found the blindfold is always necessary when you're choosing who will sit upon a throne."

Hamal tried not to twitch as a swath of heavy black fabric was tied around his head. All light vanished. He couldn't see a single particle of sand out the bottom, and with his vision gone, he imagined the desert was quieter than it had been a moment ago. But then the noise came rushing back—the strained sounds of two armies, two princes, two ready governments, two large groups of heavily armed people. Hamal could feel the tension in the air like he could feel the heat.

Whenever Cale looked at him, he could feel it. A seer's gaze was unique upon the earth, but just now, with thousands of people gathered here, it felt like a hundred seers were looking at him. All these people expected his grandfather to direct them. Hamal was glad he himself was not a reader. He tried not to squirm beneath the weight of their stares.

"Go back to your place, Seer," Shel said. "There is nothing your gift can do here."

Hamal felt Cale's hand on his shoulder, a brief touch meant to comfort him; then it disappeared, and Hamal heard his friend's boots striking hard-packed, broken soil as he walked away. The sand was different here than it had been on the battlefield. Coarser. Unyielding. An eagle cried on the wind, somewhere far above the landscape. Men in armor shifted. From a distance came the bellow of a warrior's horn, and all conversations on the sand grew silent. The event was about to begin.

Shel lifted his voice and called across the sand, "This gathering will appoint the heir of Rak-Min. The heir of blood. Those present here have agreed to the full acceptance of this man and will not protest what his blood declares. The one who does protest will do so as a traitor to the throne and will be treated as such, to the loss of rank, title, and company. Is this understood, Prince Darsek Mi-lak?"

"It is," said the prince, and his voice made Hamal shift his weight, listening. It was deeper than most voices but quiet, and it somehow reminded Hamal of the earth—of soil and growers and farming.

Shel turned. Hamal heard his boots as they adjusted on the sand. "Is this understood, Prince Gahl Tabinar?"

"It is," came the reply. The second prince had a slight lisp. Hamal could hear it clearly, and he decided the man was missing a front tooth or perhaps had a noticeable gap there.

"This is what you will see occur in your presence today," Shel continued. "The healer of the House of Rayme will set his hands upon a contingent of men whose identities are undisclosed to him, and he will announce their lineage to all gathered here. The one who is a direct descendant of Chas Rayme, the first prince of Rak-Min, will be given the throne. He will also be given both armies, immediately and without contestation, and his decisions will be final."

Shel paused. "Drake Bains and Andon Jarlek. Step forward."

Murmuring rolled through the massive crowd like a wave breaking across a sandy beach. In the midst of the muffled uproar, Hamal heard steps approaching and assumed they belonged to the men who went with those names. A short distance away, the steps stopped.

"Great knowledge has been given to both of you," Shel said. "As readers, you were born to look into history, learn from it, and give counsel to kings and princes. That is your gift and calling. However, in this matter of choosing the next prince of Rak-Min, both of you have erred."

The crowd churned again.

"One reader will be demoted in the next quarter hour. The other reader will be executed for treason."

One of the men started sputtering. The other man remained as silent as a stone.

Shel spoke over the clamor. "You know which will be demoted and which will lose his life, for one of you is just and the other is a liar." He paused, taking a breath. "If the liar is willing to take responsibility for the lives that have been lost in this struggle for power, it is possible his master will be merciful and will allow him to keep his head. Make your decision, O Reader, but do so quickly."

Hamal waited. Surely one of the readers would speak.

But no one said a word. The murmuring in the crowd died

away again, and it seemed they watched while holding their breath, so quiet the desert grew. Only the eagle spoke, calling out from where it flew above their heads.

Shel sighed deeply. "Very well. You have determined the end of your story. Let us begin. Bring forward the first man."

Footsteps advanced, a man breaking free from the ranks. Hamal listened as boots—a soldier's boots, he thought—crunched the sand and grew steadily closer until they stopped directly in front of him. Hamal reached out and touched the man, setting one hand on his chest and the other on his arm for good measure. He had learned that sometimes it was good to use both hands.

Right away, the man's bones began to speak to him.

He was twenty-one years old and a flamemaker. That latter bit of information Hamal could tell because of his body temperature. He was in prime health and used to physical labor, so Hamal decided his first thought was likely correct; this fellow was a soldier in one of the armies. He had broken five bones in his lifetime: his right shin, a bone in his hand, and three ribs. Each of these breaks had happened at separate times, and he now was as healthy as a healer.

"No," Hamal said and withdrew his hands. "This is not the one."

The man walked away, and another stepped in to take his place. When Hamal set his hands on him, he discovered he was older than the first—forty-six—and his blood eagerly told Hamal about his four children, his two grandchildren, and how pleased he was with his wife. And there was something else, something interesting: His blood was familiar. He was not a member of the House of Rayme, but he was related to someone Hamal knew.

"No, not this one either," Hamal said, "but I healed one of your relatives once. A great-great-grandfather, I think. Oh, I remember him! He was a guard in a merchant caravan, and I healed him when he fell off his horse. Pleasant man. Liked to talk about dogs. He liked dogs a great deal. Do you like dogs?"

The third man had two children and, just last year, had cracked his skull open in a fight. A healer had done a quick job healing him, and he had a thick line in his bones where the crack had been.

The fourth man had buried a wife. His bones ached with the pain of her death, and Hamal knew this man was noble and steady and the sort of soldier any captain would want. The pain in the man's bones told him so.

The fifth man had a strange rhythm in his heart. It was as if his heart were old, much older than it should have been, and it just wanted to sit down for a while. *A man with anxiety,* Hamal thought. *More anxiety than most people.*

This man needed to be healed. He obviously didn't know he had this condition, or he would have seen a healer about it, but Hamal hesitated. Several years ago he had healed a man who, much to Hamal's surprise, hadn't wanted to be healed. Ever since then, he had tried to ask first if the person wanted to be made better. But these were special circumstances and it involved the man's heart; if he didn't see a healer about this issue, it would be dangerous for him. So Hamal went ahead and healed him, encouraging his heart into a steadier, more natural rhythm. It was a simple healing, something any healer who knew what he was doing could have accomplished. *Good.* The man would feel better now and have more energy during the day. More important, his heart would not sit down when it needed to stand up.

Hamal pulled his hands away. "No, not this one either."

The words were like dry brush in a flamemaker's hands. Commotion exploded through the armies—voices, indignation, disbelief.

"This is an outrage!" one of the readers shouted. "Your

highness, you have seen my research. This is not possible. I have not failed you. It is *you*—you are the son of Rayme, just as I've told you. You cannot take this *child* seriously. Shel Galen is trying to deceive you for some reason of his own."

The man who had once been a prince of Rak-Min stood in front of Hamal in silence. He didn't move. He didn't speak. His reader shouted for nearly a full minute, saying things that were not true. They could not be true because they did not match his master's blood. This man was not of the House of Rayme, no matter what his reader declared. He was not the heir.

Eventually, the former prince sighed deeply. The air rolled out of him, and Hamal heard his boots shift on the dry ground as he turned toward his reader.

"Your highness," the reader insisted.

But his master was no longer listening to him. Hamal heard a sharp metallic rasp, and the reader's voice jumped, hitting higher notes.

"Shel Galen," the former prince said, and Hamal recognized his deep, earthy voice. This was Darsek Mi-lak, the one who had attacked Emia and her team. The one who was stealing people so they could be part of his army. He had gone to great lengths to take the throne he thought was his. "Is this man the liar?"

"Yes, he is," Shel replied.

Hamal sensed a rush of movement, and the reader's frantic voice cut off. An instant blanket of quiet, odd in its strength, fell across the desert. No one moved for a long time.

"Bring the next man," Shel Galen said.

The next man, man number six, was missing one of the toes on his left foot.

The seventh man had a noticeable gap between his front teeth, and Hamal knew this was Gahl Tabinar, the second prince. He was young—several years younger than Darsek Mi-lak—and had never broken a bone in his life. But he had been stabbed once in the chest and another time in the stomach, and his muscled arms bore a few thin scars like those a blade would make. He had allowed the wounds on his arms to heal on their own and hadn't bothered to see a healer.

As Hamal listened to the man's body and heard the story of his blood, he decided he was a man who was willing to take certain risks but not others. He had a type of wisdom, and Hamal thought it probable that Cale would like him. They would be friends. Cale liked people who showed they were wise.

But one thing was surprising. Hamal stood there, his right hand on Gahl Tabinar's chest and his left on the fellow's arm, and he didn't know what to say.

"No," he said at last, reaching up to rub the top of his head because he didn't understand. "This one isn't the heir either."

As confusion swept the sand, Shel Galen said calmly, "Bring the next man."

"The next man?" Darsek Mi-lak repeated. "But there are no others, Shel. Clearly, you know what occurs here more than we do. If Tabinar is not the heir either, then hundreds of people have died for naught, and both of us were deceived."

Shel agreed. "Yes, you were. Bring the next man."

The eighth man had knobs on his knees—bony parts that stuck out and likely caused him knee pain when he ran for long distances. Hamal didn't ask if he wanted to be healed either; he just assumed he did because this man was a soldier, too. He got rid of the bony parts for him, erasing them from his system before sending him on his way.

The ninth man was Cale.

Hamal started laughing. "This certainly is not the heir of the House of Rayme."

Cale patted him on the shoulder before walking away.

The tenth man was a boy no older than Hamal. His body had seen much trauma in his short lifetime: dozens of broken bones and muscles that had been bruised and sliced open before being healed. He had been beaten over and over again, but talented healers had put him back together and kept him alive. For the last several months, he had been healthy, and he was stronger now than he was even a year ago.

Hamal paused, his hands on the boy.

More than these things, more than the sorrow in his bones or the pain he had endured, stronger than any of those stories—his blood spoke in a familiar voice. Hamal knew his blood. He *knew* him.

"This is him!" Hamal exclaimed, gripping the boy's arm. "This is him! This is the heir! This is the one you want."

Grinning widely, he pulled off his blindfold, blinked against the sunlight, and sucked in a surprised breath as he realized he was looking into a face he knew.

It was Tell.

The boy who worked for Shel Galen. The one Shel had purchased from a slaver.

20 A Matter of Justice

That night while the sun sank behind the western hills of Morden's Passage and the stars came out, Hamal sat in the sand with new companions and thought about the House of Rayme.

The House of Rayme was famous across the continent. Morden, the first king of King's Barrow, was the main person people thought about whenever the House of Rayme was mentioned. Tell descended from Chas, one of Morden's brothers, while Cedrick, the current king of King's Barrow, was a descendant of Morden himself. This made Tell the king's cousin. Anywhere he went on the continent, Tell would be treated with great honor.

Hamal nearly laughed. No wonder Cale thought Tell seemed familiar to him! He was the king's cousin, just like Satha was the king's cousin. Truly, Cale was a talented seer.

"Where did you find him?" Darsek Mi-lak asked from the other side of the fire.

Supper had started just a few moments ago, delivered in a giant iron pot by the military kitchen staff. Hamal held a bowl of stew in his hands, and he was waiting for it to cool. He smelled it and determined there was going to be a lot of pepper, which was common in Dasken. Everything was hot here: the sun, the sand, the tempers, the food.

As he ate, Shel explained, "I found him in a little village in Ar Pik. Bought him for three torrin."

Darsek made a noise in the back of his throat.

Gahl Tabinar muttered through his mouthful of stew, "By the gods."

Hamal leaned close to Cale and whispered, "It has been several months since I purchased anything in Dasken. How much is three torrin?"

Cale tapped the bowl in Hamal's hands with one finger. "It would buy you supper in King's Barrow."

Hamal looked down into his stew. "Only one supper?"

"Yes."

"Well, that's not very much, is it?"

"No, it isn't," Cale agreed and laughed quietly. "Your grandfather bought a prince with a bowl of stew."

Shel pointed his spoon at Cale. "No, I did not buy a prince. On the contrary, I bought a miserable, self-focused, silent slave boy who called himself Lost. That's what I bought. Took him a full week to answer when I asked him a question and another month before he told me his real name. If he'd had his way, he would have thrown himself off the southern cliffs and considered it a benefit to mankind. But we kept an eye on him, and he eventually had a change of heart."

Sitting next to Shel on the same blanket, Tell grunted. He didn't protest or argue, but his answer—that one sound— communicated a great deal and Hamal grinned, unable to help himself. Shel had a similar reaction. He put his head back and laughed until he had to rub his eyes.

"You needed some persuasion, son. What else could I have done? You can question my methods if you like, but I am quite pleased with the final result. Any other feeler would have required years of training, but a boy named Intelligence? Six months. It was simple. You made it simple for us."

Tell kept eating. His manner suggested he'd heard all these words before. With everyone watching him in silence, it was like his simple activity was the most fascinating thing any of them had seen in a year.

"So you bought a slave boy in Ar Pik," Tabinar said. "When did you discover he was the heir to the throne?"

Darsek replied, "I wager he knew from the beginning. This is Shel Galen, the sage of Dasken. What is hidden from him?"

But Shel shook his head. "I didn't know—not in the beginning. I wondered; that was all. Some of his mannerisms seemed familiar to me, but I couldn't have told you why, for I knew I had never seen this child before. Tell looks like his mother, a woman who died several years ago, but he acts like his father, a man he never met. This is because the House of Rayme is powerful on the earth. That is what the gods desired for them, and so they made their legacy strong. There are signs of that strength everywhere you look—if you are familiar with them and know how to weigh them. There were signs with Tell, strong signs, though he resisted them at every turn." Shel smiled broadly. "He resisted all the way into Theraine, when we took him to visit the prophet."

Cale straightened up.

Gregory stopped writing.

Tabinar stopped eating, which was something of a feat.

"You took him to see the prophet," Darsek said with noticeable interest in his voice.

Shel nodded. "Aye. The prophet is the one who confirmed Tell's heritage. Not to me, but to Tell. He told Tell he is the son of Tallus Rayme, whose recent assassination stunned all of Dasken.

Tell is the only survivor among Tallus's sons. Indeed, he is alive in part because his enemy did not believe he should be concerned with a boy, a slave, who called himself Lost."

Shel's eyes gleamed in the firelight. "The assassin knew of Tell's mother and the possibility of a secret heir, so he hunted him." He paused in an obvious show of drama and made them wait as he continued eating. "He actually came to see us one night, when we were still in Ra-Faal."

"When was this?" Darsek demanded.

Shel shrugged one shoulder. "About two weeks after he killed Tallus. We had a fine supper, all three of us together, and the man changed his mind about killing Tell and went away again."

Everyone, Hamal included, stared at Shel.

"He *changed his mind*," Darsek repeated.

Tell made that sound again, the one that suggested more was happening than Hamal understood. "That isn't exactly what happened, Shel."

Hamal leaned forward eagerly and asked, "What *did* happen?" He loved stories like this, when his grandfather did something no one expected and could not have predicted. Of course, when he thought about it, he supposed all his grandfather's stories were like this one—unexpected things.

Tell was the one who answered. "He threatened him."

"I did not," Shel replied. He was laughing so hard that he was having trouble doing anything else. Hamal sensed his utter joy. "We had a simple, easy conversation about how he shouldn't kill the boy I had purchased, that I wished to keep him alive. The assassin came to agree with me, and he left."

Tell was shaking his head. "You told him that he was going to die if he didn't act with wisdom. That is what you said, and it sounded like a threat to me. His face changed colors and he looked ill, and he nearly dropped his spoon. *He* knew he was being threatened, even if you pretend otherwise."

"I pretend nothing!" Shel chortled.

"Did you know he was there to kill you, Tell?" Hamal asked and only afterward thought about how he should refer to him by title. Tell was the ruler of Rak-Min now, not a slave. No one would ever call him *Lost* again.

"Not at the time," Tell replied easily. He didn't seem to mind that Hamal had called him by his name. "However, I came to understand soon afterward."

"You determined the truth for yourself," Shel said, nodding proudly. "Because you are wise."

"Because I am not an idiot," Tell replied.

Shel and several of the others chuckled. "Wisdom and idiocy are two separate things. This is true even when they travel the same road for a time."

Tabinar had nearly emptied his bowl. He ate like a man who thought he would never eat again. Servants in military uniform quickly stepped forward to fill his bowl as he said, "The assassin was tracked and captured. Lost his head like the wretched murderer he was." He paused to watch as a servant added another ladle of stew into his bowl. "Your council, your highness, will support you fully. We never should have listened to the possibility that we were somehow associated with the mighty House of Rayme. The moment the idea was presented to us, it should have seemed like foolishness, quite as it does now. In truth, it is astonishing how a reader can lead you to believe something that is actually a lie."

Gregory's pencil hesitated on its page.

Darsek sighed. "For once in my life, Tabinar, I fear I must agree with you."

As the conversation continued, Hamal leaned up against Cale's arm and whispered, "He is not Lost anymore." Those words seemed important in this moment. *He is not Lost.*

Cale smiled. "No, he isn't."

Halfway through the meal, one of the prince's first commands came to pass. The jeweler named Krasak was brought to them in chains.

He was smaller than Hamal thought he would be. For some reason, he had been picturing a giant of a man, someone who looked capable of theft and murder. This was just a man and he was small. Krasak's lip was bleeding, and the skin around his left eye was black and swollen. Hamal gathered he had resisted those who had come to collect him. The man kept his gaze on the ground and refused to look at anyone. He stood in perfect silence, as if he refused to believe this was happening to him. It could be this way with jewelers sometimes. Sometimes they were so committed to their goal that they did not understand when they had done something wrong.

"Where was he?" Darsek growled to his men.

"Hiding in a trunk," his captain replied and nodded to Cale, "just as his lordship said he would be."

"I have kept detailed records, your highness," Darsek told Tell. "Every person Krasak has delivered to me will be located and presented to you by morning. I will compensate them for their time and supply them with an additional bonus of my own accord, as a sign of my good will."

The same case, Hamal thought, and for the first time, he clearly understood why the prophet had said such a thing. Shel Galen's case and their case—it was the same case in the end. Darsek had welcomed Krasak into his military, but he'd quickly given him up when the prince ordered it. Tell had also spoken to Darsek about the members of his military who were from King's Barrow, and those Krasak had stolen were going home. They were able to go home. Hamal thought of Justice, and what he wanted to do in South Barrow, and how pleased he would be that his people had returned. *It is the same case in the end.*

There was only one thing Hamal still wondered about.

"I say, Cale," Hamal whispered.

Cale turned to him.

"Have you heard about anything silver? What have we seen that is silver but is worth more than gold?" Hamal looked at the men gathered around the fire—very powerful men, all of them, though in different ways—and shook his head. "I cannot think of anything, but the prophet thinks this is important. For Justice."

"The prophet's message to you," Cale murmured. He, too, looked around at the members of Tell's council. "I have not seen anything. Not yet. It remains a mystery, one we will need to answer soon, for we are scheduled to leave in the morning."

"Perhaps it will happen on the way back," Hamal suggested. "The prophet didn't say *when* it would happen, just that it would."

Cale nodded. "We will see."

21 The Unexpected Worth of Silver

Thirty-four. That was the number of people Krasak had captured in South Barrow and sold to Darsek Mi-lak, and thirty-four was the number of people Hamal, Cale, and the others took home with them.

The youngest person in the group was a boy of fourteen; the oldest was a man of fifty-four. Hamal laid his hands on every person in the group and made certain all of them were in the best of health. Though military healers had looked at each of them, he still found some joints that needed repairing and some issues with bones, and the fifty-four-year-old had scarring in his lungs from an infection when he was a boy. Hamal couldn't do much with scarring, but he could *rearrange* the scarring so it caused the man less trouble.

"There now," he said, patting the man on the shoulder. "How does that feel?"

The man took a deep breath and stopped. He let it out hurriedly and did it again, drawing in air until he couldn't possibly draw in any more. He looked at Hamal and blinked once, then again, and then several times in a row. "I have not been able to draw a breath without pain since I was a child."

Hamal smiled. "Now you can be a child again."

They said goodbye to Hamal's grandfather and the new prince of Rak-Min and traveled north on the same road they had taken yesterday, traversing the outer regions of Morden's Passage. On the banks of the South River, they waited for their turn on the ferry and Hamal said goodbye to Ji. She was wearing the *bassan* again, which protected everything but her face and hands from the sharp heat of the sun. He remembered the tattoos on her arms and wished they'd had more time to talk about them—to talk about anything. This trip into Dasken ended up being quite short.

"It was a pleasure to watch you work," Ji told Hamal and shook his hand soberly.

As she touched him, the sadness in her bones nearly took his breath. There was a story here; he could tell. This was pain that had lasted a long time and had been hard for her to endure. Her bones recorded what had happened to her, both the good parts and the bad parts, the happy things and the sad things.

"Perhaps we will have the opportunity to work together in the future," she said.

"I hope so," he replied and meant it in his heart.

She nodded once, released his hand, and walked away.

Gregory took her place soon after she had gone, and they watched as Ji and the rest of her team departed. "An interesting girl, that," the reader said when nothing more could be seen of them but a cloud of sand drifting down the road.

"I think so, too," Hamal answered.

"I was able to discover a few things about her," Gregory offered and began to supply details. "She was born a slave, but her master was a betting man, and when she was fifteen, she made a wager with him and won. He fulfilled his bargain and gave her her freedom. She went on to win the Blood Race—she is the first woman in seventy years to do so—and turned down several offers of employment from people of much more renown than Emia. Emia was her choice."

Hamal glanced at him. How had Gregory managed to discover so much about Ji in a short period of time? Which person on her team had he asked? Ji wouldn't have told him. At least Hamal didn't think so. She seemed quite private.

As Hamal wondered about these things and marveled at how a reader could uncover secrets, a new thought dropped into his head. He had already asked Cale, but Gregory would be a good one to ask, too. Readers knew things, and—clearly—they knew how to find things out.

"In all your research and note-taking during this journey, have you heard of something silver? Anything silver, even something small. The prophet left a message for me with Ambassador Torrek, and he talked about finding something that was silver or had something to do with silver, and it would be important for Justice Ashby. So has anyone said anything about silver?"

Gregory stared at him until Hamal shifted awkwardly and asked, "What is it?"

"She grew up in a silver mine," the reader answered.

"Who grew up in a silver mine?"

"Ji. The young lady of whom we are speaking." When Hamal just gaped at him, Gregory cleared his throat and began the story. "She worked with her parents in a silver mine until one of the shafts collapsed, and her parents and half the other workers were killed. That is why her master allowed her to make such a wager with him. He gave her the opportunity to prove herself because of her parents. It was, perhaps, an odd type of compassion, but I believe that is the correct word for it."

"A silver mine."

"Yes."

"She grew up in a silver mine."

"Yes, Hamal," Gregory said patiently. "In horrific conditions, I imagine. Have you ever seen a mine? It is no place for a child. Not even one who can heal herself. I once read a book written by the owner of Black Hook Mine, that famous mine in the Bralin province, and he said—"

Hamal whirled around and faced the road. Dust still lingered in the air. It was the only sign that Ji and her team had gone that direction. They were getting away.

Ji was getting away.

"Cale!" Hamal shouted. "Cale, I know what the silver is!"

One of the weathermakers called to them.

Thunder rumbled in a clear sky. Hamal, Cale, Gregory, and two weathermaker guards rode for a mile before they rounded the next hill, and there they were—Emia and her team, waiting in the middle of the road.

"We have a contract, and I was hoping to reach our destination on time," Emia stated from the back of her horse.

As Cale began to explain the situation, Hamal slid out of the saddle and stumbled up to Ji. "Ji," he panted, his heart running. "Do you know...Justice Ashby?"

She looked at him blankly. "No, I do not."

"Oh, oh! What's his other name? Why does he have to have two names? Justice Hewen! Do you know Justice Hewen?"

For a moment, she did not respond one way or another. She just sat there in the saddle and looked at him.

"Ji?" he prodded.

The muscles tightened in her jaw. "No, I don't know him either."

Hamal stared up at her. "Why—why are you saying that? That

isn't true. You *do* know him." On the way, Gregory had helped Hamal put the pieces together, and Hamal said now, "He ran in the Blood Race with you, didn't he? He has *almost* as many birds on his arms as you do, but he didn't win—you did. You were the Crown Holder that year, just like you told me. Yes, you do know him. Why would you say you didn't?"

With a deep sigh, Ji swung her leg around and dropped from the saddle, so she could stand in front of Hamal on the road. He could hear her heartbeat. It ran like mad, and all at once, he realized it didn't matter what she said to him. He knew the truth. Her heart had told him, and she didn't need to use words.

"It doesn't matter, Hamal." She spoke quietly, and he had to lean closer because he could barely understand her. "Yes, I know Justice Hewen. Yes, I outran him in the Blood Race. But we are not friends."

Hamal lowered his voice as well. "Does he love you?"

She scoffed. "No."

Hamal didn't understand. He realized he was rubbing the top of his head again, and he made himself stop, lowering his hand to his side. "No, I think he loves you." When she scowled, he said quickly, "The Prophet of Theraine told me you are worth more than gold to him, to Justice. What does that mean if it does *not* mean he loves you? How can you be worth more than gold to someone if love is not involved? You matter to him."

She looked away. "Hamal…"

"Tell me what happened, Ji. Why are you angry with him?"

Her eyes brewed with flamemaker fury. She was not a flamemaker, but just now Hamal could imagine she was. "I am not going to have this conversation with you."

"But it is wise to have this conversation with me. Something is not right here, and I want to do for Justice what he has done for many, many others. I want to make things right for him. Tell me."

A long moment passed.

"Very well," Ji hissed at last. "If the sage insists."

Hamal flinched at her tone.

"I thought highly of Justice Hewen for a time, but I do not think this way anymore. We made an arrangement to meet, and he didn't come. I think I can tell when a man is in love with me, Hamal, and I can tell when he isn't. It was the making of fools anyway. I barely knew him."

"When was he supposed to meet you?"

"Excuse me?"

"When, Ji? Was it in the last four months?"

She hesitated, and Hamal squeezed his hands together until the knuckles turned colors. He couldn't help it. He couldn't stay still.

"Ji—*chila*. Justice Hewen has been in prison for the last four months for hitting a city patrolman. That bad man we arrested last night? Justice found out that Krasak was selling the king's people to Darsek Mi-lak, and he became angry and hit him. He was in prison for four months before we could get him out. That is why he didn't meet you. That is the only reason he didn't make it. He *couldn't* make it."

Hamal reached down and grabbed her hand. This was the woman with the sad bones. This was the one who had lost her parents as a child and had to battle for her freedom, because no one else was there to battle for her. She had battled and she had won.

"You," he told her, "are a warrior. That is how you are made. You need to think like a warrior now. Your friendship with Justice is something worth fighting for. Fight for this. This is important."

She looked at him and didn't say a word.

22 When They Came Home Again

When you worked for a king, you couldn't just go home and sleep. You had plenty of important things to do.

You had to fill out written reports so the palace knew all the things you accomplished while you were away. You had to go speak to the king and tell him your story, even though Gregory Almes's reports were sitting on his desk right there in plain view, and they were much more detailed than anything you remembered. You had to talk about the prophet and why you thought he went home instead of seeing you. Yes, you knew him, and if you had thought it was important, you would have said something.

And—this was the most important of all—you needed to take all thirty-four people back to their homes and write down their addresses, so servants in the palace could take care of them, bring them any supplies they needed, and make sure they knew the king wanted to help them. Cedrick was a mystery to Hamal in many ways, but in one way he was as clear as the summer sun in Dasken. Hamal could hear the king's heartbeat when he spoke of his missing people, those who had been sold in Dasken and those who had been shipped north to the mine, and Hamal knew how upset all of this made him. Cedrick was a good king. He was also a good man.

By the time everything was taken care of, two full days had passed. Finally, after supper and during a thunderstorm that didn't drop any rain, Hamal and Cale went to see Justice.

The feeler had moved back into his family house on Newbold Street. It was a large house with several balconies and a porch up on the roof. When they arrived, Justice was going over project plans with his architect, Corin Groff. One of the councilmen, a reader, was there as well, and Hamal took this to be a good sign. Why would a councilman be here after dinner unless he liked Justice and approved of him? This was good.

"Welcome back to the king's land," Justice greeted in his deep, familiar voice that always made Hamal feel safe and protected. He embraced Hamal and shook Cale's hand, and Hamal felt as if they had known one another for several years, not just a few days. "We heard of your success within an hour of your ship's arrival. Well done. Sincerely…well done. You brought back every single one of them."

"We had some help," Hamal said.

"Oh, yes—the prophet. What was that like?" Justice chuckled and his brows lifted. "I have heard several unique stories about him. They say he can be difficult to understand. Because of his gift. Did you find this to be true?"

"Yes, he is always difficult to understand, but you don't mind it because it is an adventure and a mystery. The words he says are good words, even if you don't understand them." Hamal glanced at Cale. "But we didn't get to see the prophet this time. He sent for us, but he left before we could get there. Instead, he gave us a riddle and, well, it was about you."

Justice paused. "About me?"

Behind him, Groff and the councilman exchanged a look.

The councilman reached into an inner pocket and brought out a small notebook, just like a reader would do. Following the book, he withdrew a short, stubby pencil and waited expectantly.

Cale spoke for the first time since entering the room. "You did not tell us you were recently in Dasken." He was watching Justice.

"I was not recently in Dasken," Justice replied.

Hamal twitched, while Cale studied Justice with narrowed eyes.

"An interesting assessment," the seer murmured.

"But you *were* in Dasken," Hamal said, trying to get the feeler to explain himself. Why was it so hard to get Justice to talk? "We know you were."

Justice sighed and sat back down in his chair, folding his hands in his lap. Somehow the motion made him seem kingly. How could folding your hands make you appear like a king? Hamal was certain that when *he* folded his hands, he did not give the same impression.

"It was thirteen months ago. I do not consider it recent," Justice replied.

"What did you do while you were there?" Hamal asked.

"I was traveling in Rak-Min with my cousin and my friend Steadfast. It was a short trip, less than two weeks. We tried the food, tasted the ale, and rejoiced in our temporary freedom from the university. It was a pleasant venture. Brief but pleasant." Justice smiled politely. "What does this have to do with the Prophet of Theraine?"

Cale looked at Hamal and lifted his hand in a motion that greatly resembled a shrug. They had talked about this on the ship, and every time Cale had used the same words: "It was a message for *you*, Hamal. If wisdom wishes to fiddle with a man's love life, it is best if he does it by himself."

Hamal took a small step forward and tried not to twitch again. "Justice."

"Yes?"

"Did anything of importance happen while you were in Dasken?"

And that, finally, was when Hamal heard it—the sudden stumble in the big fellow's heart.

Brief but pleasant. The words were wrong. They were moonlight in sunshine, a cold wind in the Dasken desert. They did not fit what else Hamal could suddenly hear: a thunder of sound where there had been only relaxed quiet a moment ago. Justice's heart spoke in this room the way Ji's heart had spoken in the desert, saying many words that did not cross the lips. How was it that two people could find themselves in the same place, but they were together and apart at the same time? It did not make sense to Hamal. Someday when he met the woman he loved, he would just tell her. He would use words and tell her, so she would not have any doubts.

Justice looked at Hamal for a long time, his heart rumbling like a weathermaker's call. He was not smiling now. "Yes."

"Did you find something in Dasken that was worth more than gold?"

Justice stood up slowly. "Yes."

"And did you miss an appointment with this thing that is worth more than gold, because you were in prison and you didn't know how to reach her?"

The feeler seemed to lose his air. His shoulders hunched and his voice quieted. "Yes."

Hamal glanced at Groff and the councilman. One was openly staring. The other was writing madly in his book. It occurred to Hamal that as Justice was a feeler, he might want to keep certain things to himself, and it might be hard for him to do—*because* he was a feeler. So Hamal said to him, "I need to see you out in the hallway. Privately."

Groff and the councilman both started frowning.

Justice followed Hamal out of the room. The feeler pulled the door shut behind him, and as soon as the latch clicked into place, he began speaking in a whisper. "What was the message, Hamal? And why would a well-known man like the Prophet of Theraine deign to—"

His words trickled away. He froze, his hand still on the door handle.

She was standing in his hallway.

She wore a *tristant*, a type of Dasken dress that had trousers underneath, and Hamal wanted to laugh because it was like she thought she might need to run away, and this was her running uniform. It seemed to him that it would be much easier to run in a *tristant* than it would be in a regular King's Barrow dress. It was blue. She looked nice in blue, and Hamal had told her so.

Neither person moved. Justice stood like a statue made of iron, his hand wrapped around the door handle as if his palm were nailed there. Ji, meanwhile, reminded Hamal of a desert cat, watching to see which way the other animal would turn.

"Ji," Justice whispered.

As he said her name, the muscles tightened in her throat, and her voice was barely a breath. "You didn't come."

He didn't seem to hear the words. "Ji," he said again.

She lifted her chin and shifted in her boots. The lamplight washed across her arms and made the birds tattooed there appear to move on their own power. "I expected never to see you again."

Justice started shaking his head. "That was never going to happen. Not even for a moment. You would have seen me."

Her eyes narrowed. "Coming here was not my idea."

Again, Justice seemed to miss the words. Or perhaps the

feeler somehow heard other words, something Hamal didn't hear at all. "I can't think of anything without thinking of you. I meant what I told you. Every word. By the gods, Ji. How is it you are here? How is it you—?"

She moved first. But he moved quickly afterward.

Hamal averted his gaze and decided he should leave, but they were blocking the door, so he sneaked down the hall and sat by himself in the library for a little while. He smiled the entire time and thought the Prophet of Theraine quite wise indeed.

For two days, things were rather quiet in the city of King's Barrow. On the first night, Justice and Ji came to dinner at Cale and Satha's house. Justice held Ji's hand almost the entire time, and he spoke more words than Hamal had ever heard from him. He talked a lot.

On the second night, Hamal didn't go to sleep until three in the morning because he started thinking about bones, and sometimes when he started thinking about bones, he forgot to do other things.

On the third day, they were summoned to the palace.

Hamal, Cale, and Justice met with the king in his study. It was about six o'clock in the evening, and a council meeting had just ended. As the others began talking about the latest weather predictions—a point of interest because the palace weathermakers were warning of a drought—Hamal sat on the couch along the wall and thought about the thing he'd been thinking about all day. His head was full of bones. Bones and more bones, and how they worked, and how they could be put back together.

"You are very quiet this evening, Hamal," the king observed.

Hamal looked up and realized everyone was watching him. "Oh, I'm sorry. I will talk if you would like me to, your majesty."

A corner of the king's mouth rose. "I confess I am still surprised that you knew the Prophet of Theraine and never said a word about it. Is there anything else about the prophet you have somehow *forgotten* to mention?"

Hamal considered the question seriously. It was good to take a king's question, hold it with care, and examine it from all angles. "Well, your majesty, I know the Prophet of Theraine is very old."

The king nodded. Hamal noticed the corner of his mouth was still twitching, but he couldn't imagine why, because Hamal had answered the question in all earnestness.

"I imagine that is true," the king replied somberly. "He has been the Prophet of Theraine since my grandfather's time."

"Oh, since long before that. He is the oldest of us." No one said anything, so Hamal continued, "He actually moved to Theraine before there was a Theraine. He's a prophet, you know, and he knew where he was supposed to be, so he went there and waited for the Theranians to come. When they came, they killed all the dragons that lived in the jungles, and the prophet has lived in the same little house for many years, right next door to his friend the ambassador."

Silence filled the room.

"Wait," Cale began.

The king leaned forward. "*Before* Theraine existed...?"

"Did you say dragons?" Justice asked.

Cale stood up from his chair and looked at Hamal. "The oldest *of us*? Is the Prophet of Theraine a sage? Hamal..."

Hamal nodded. "He's my grandfather's brother. His older brother. We call him the Prophet of Theraine because that's what everyone calls him, but sometimes when I am visiting him, I call him Uncle Kent. His real name, of course, is Kentarinti'Lanak—he was named after a star, you know—but no one ever calls him that. It's too hard to say. It's easier just to call him *the prophet* and be done with it."

"He's a sage," the king stated.

Hamal shrugged, a little uncertain about the king's tone of voice. "Well…yes. I thought you knew." He looked over at Cale, who was still just standing there. "Didn't you know? Whenever people say the Prophet of Theraine, they don't mean *many* prophets, as if there's been more than one. They mean just one, who has been the Prophet of Theraine the whole time. It's the same person. Really, Cale, I thought you knew. Are there other things you don't know?"

"Most likely," Cale muttered.

"He's a sage," the king said again. "They've had a sage longer than we have."

Everyone has had a sage longer than you have, Hamal thought but he didn't say it because he thought it might be rude. He had known Cale for less than two months. That was not a long time at all.

"But this doesn't make sense," the king said. "I thought sages avoided cities. Your father, Hamal—didn't you say he lives near Jessen Springs, but he stays out of the city as much as he possibly can?"

"Yes, that's true. He likes small towns, if he goes into a town at all. Many sages are the same way."

"Then what does that mean for you? What does it mean for Shel Galen?" The king started frowning. "I know what people call him—the sage of Dasken. If your grandfather is the sage of Dasken, and your uncle is the sage of Theraine, then what does that make you?"

Hamal smiled. That was a simple question, one that came with a simple answer. "Dasken isn't mine and Theraine isn't mine, but I like King's Barrow. King's Barrow is different for me. I think I will stay here for a long time, because it is a good place to stay."

23 Until Next Time

That night on the way back to the house, Hamal took a deep breath and said, "Cale, I've been thinking a lot about bones."

"Bones," Cale repeated from the other side of the coach.

"Aye. Bones. And sometimes when I start thinking about things, I find that I can do things I couldn't do before. I have an answer I didn't realize I had. We just came back from Dasken, and I healed many people in Dasken—I healed some bones while we were down there."

"And you think you might know something you didn't know before? About bones?"

"That is exactly what I mean."

Cale watched him in shadows that changed as the coach passed beneath street lamps and lines of tiny lights hung in trees. Warm, orange light fell across Cale's arms and shoulders and then rolled away. "Do sages grow in their gifts the way other gifts do? Do you get better at healing with time? I have difficulty imagining this."

"Oh, yes. All the time. Sages, perhaps, grow more than all the other gifts. We need to grow more." Hamal laughed.

Cale did not laugh.

Scooting to the edge of the seat, Hamal said, "So I have been thinking of something. Give me your hand, please."

Cale blinked once—slowly, as if surprised—and lifted his left hand, the one he depended on because the other one gave him trouble.

Hamal stopped him. "No, not that one. The injured one. The one those bad men crushed with a hammer." He nodded. "I want to try something."

Cale grew still. He looked at Hamal for a long moment. Without a word, he stretched out his arm, offering the hand that had been injured, the one Hamal had not been able to heal completely.

Hamal took it and he tried something.

For a moment, everything was quiet as the coach continued down the street.

Then Cale drew a quick breath. Hamal glanced up in time to see his friend's expression, his first response, as he flexed his fingers.

Hamal smiled and released Cale's hand, satisfied at last.

Look for book 3 in the Hamal Books

The Healer Who Didn't Remember

Coming fall 2018

Acknowledgements

Many thanks to Trace Chiodo, designer extraordinaire, for being my work buddy and listening to me when I'm trying to figure something out. And I'm trying to figure out a lot of things these days!

Thanks to Jane Lambert, Jennifer Stapleton, Brooke Walsh, Cherish Brunner, Susan Stinton, and Michelle Cornellier for their help with Hamal's ongoing story. Thanks also to my sister-in-law, Carla Stinton, and her marvelous calligraphy that makes the Hamal Books look so cool.

And thank you to my readers who have been with me in this process. This book started as an online serial novel, and you guys provided faithful support! Now here is the finished product in all its glory, and you played a role in seeing it birthed. Thanks to all of you—particularly Jill Blovits and Corrie Groff, whose names appear in this story.

Or a creative, you're-in-a-fantasy-world-now version of your names.

If you love Hamal,
get more of his story!

Visit

TheHamalbooks.com